PROJECT FAIRY

JACQUELINE WILSON

Illustrated by *Rachael Dean*

PUFFIN

PUFFIN BOOKS

UK | USA | Canada | Ireland | Australia
India | New Zealand | South Africa

Puffin Books is part of the Penguin Random House group of companies
whose addresses can be found at global.penguinrandomhouse.com.

www.penguin.co.uk
www.puffin.co.uk
www.ladybird.co.uk

First published 2022
This edition published 2023
003

Text copyright © Jacqueline Wilson, 2022
Illustrations copyright © Rachael Dean, 2022

The moral right of the author and illustrator has been asserted

Text design by Janene Spencer
Printed and bound in Great Britain by Clays Ltd, Elcograf S.p.A.

The authorized representative in the EEA is Penguin Random House Ireland,
Morrison Chambers, 32 Nassau Street, Dublin D02 YH68

A CIP catalogue record for this book is available from the British Library

ISBN: 978–0–241–56716–6

All correspondence to:
Puffin Books
Penguin Random House Children's
One Embassy Gardens
8 Viaduct Gardens
London SW11 7BW

MIX
Paper from
responsible sources
FSC
www.fsc.org
FSC® C018179

Penguin Random House is committed to a
sustainable future for our business, our readers
and our planet. This book is made from Forest
Stewardship Council® certified paper.

For Trish
Bindweed is the bane of her life

CHAPTER ONE

You'll never guess what my mum gave me for a birthday present. She came into my bedroom carrying breakfast on a tray, with my little brother Robin singing 'Happy Birthday' at the top of his voice. It was a special treat breakfast – orange juice and toast with strawberry jam cut into heart shapes. It's a Mum thing. She handed me the pink tissue parcel so eagerly, her eyes shining.

I felt the paper carefully. There was something soft folded up inside. Clothes.

I hadn't really wanted clothes. I'd wanted an electric scooter most of all, but a bike or skateboard would have been

fine as well. They probably cost too much even second-hand, so then I'd have liked one of those giant sets of felt-tip pens and a sketch pad. I didn't want a special colouring book because I prefer making up my own pictures. I like drawing outer space and jungles and wild animals.

If I had to have clothes, then I wanted a really cool T-shirt, maybe black with a gorilla on it. Or a skeleton, or a grinning face, or a cartoon character. I felt very anxious about Mum's choice. She's very much a pink person. She once bought me a candyfloss-pink T-shirt with *Mummy's Girl* written on it in fancy white lettering. I nearly died.

I slipped my hand inside the tissue. It didn't feel like a T-shirt. There was a smooth silky bit and then something like net, all puffed up. I felt sick. It seemed to be a party frock. It was totally the wrong sort of present for me. I didn't go to any parties for a start. Nobody invites me now.

I don't care. Well, I suppose I do a bit, but I actually hate parties, especially the sort where you dress up in your best clothes. A party dress would be my worst-ever outfit.

Maybe Mum thought I didn't go to parties because I didn't have a proper dress. I tried hard to get my face into a happy, thrilled expression. I didn't want to hurt her.

'Ooh, I think I've guessed what it is!' I said, trying to make my voice sound pleased.

Mum smiled at me.

'What is it, what is it, what is it?' Robin asked, jumping up and down eagerly on my bed.

I took a deep breath and ripped open the pink tissue. A dress fell out. Not a party dress. It was far far worse. It was a *fairy* frock. It had a pale pink silky bodice attached to a froth of deep pink net, six layers of it, so it stuck out in all directions. And there were wings attached to the back of the bodice, floppy feathery wings.

Perhaps some girls might long for such a dress. Maybe very *little* girls. But I thought this fairy outfit the most startlingly horrible garment I'd ever seen. I was so taken aback I couldn't think of a thing to say. I just froze, my mouth open.

Robin was impressed. 'Oh, Mum, it's a fairy dress! With wings! You'll be able to fly now, Mab!'

He wasn't teasing. He seriously seemed to think I could spread those false wings and fly out of the window.

'Mab will be able to fly in her dreams,' said Mum, clasping her hands. 'You do like it, don't you, darling?'

I swallowed. 'It's . . . lovely,' I said, straining to sound convincing. 'Where did you get it?'

'I was looking up fairy dust online, wanting to order some more for your birthday,' said Mum. (Fairy dust is this sparkly sequin stuff that Mum sprinkles everywhere on special occasions. She puts it in birthday cards and Christmas cards too so you have to open them very carefully – and even then you get fairy dust flying everywhere and you discover the odd sequin about your person for days afterwards.) 'Then I noticed that Google was asking if I wanted to look up fairy *dress* and so I did, and I immediately knew I had to buy you one for your birthday! I did wonder if I should ask you first, because I know you mostly like your jeans and T-shirts, but who wouldn't want their own actual fairy dress?' said Mum.

I wouldn't! I screamed inside, but I grinned valiantly.

I hate upsetting Mum. It's so easy to make her cry. She was very ill after Dad walked out when Robin was a toddler – only two and a half! She was in hospital for quite a while and Robin and I had to go into care. For a whole year! We had a very kind foster mum but she wasn't *our* mum. We minded terribly. I was already missing my dad but I missed Mum even more.

She got better and finally, after we'd had lots of visits and some weekends with Mum, our social worker said we could go and live with her again. That was last summer, more than a year ago now. We moved right away for a fresh start. Mum got a job in a supermarket, so we get discount food, and our new flat doesn't cost much because it's social housing. I had to start at a new school. It was OK at first because I made friends with Billie, but then she palled up with Cathy and Anita at the end of last term and now they are my deadly enemies. It's horrible, but the only thing that really matters is that Robin and I are back together with Mum.

She's mostly fine now, but she still gets upset easily. She cries at the silliest things, even happy things like those cute kitten clips on YouTube. And she gets obsessed with stuff. She watches television a lot. She loves *Escape to the Country* and checks out every house as if she's considering it for us, even though we couldn't possibly afford it and she's terrified of cows anyway. Her favourite programme in all the world is *Strictly Come Dancing.* She's learned how to do the old-fashioned waltz and whirls Robin or me round and round our little living room until we get dizzy.

She loves making scrapbooks and photo albums, and taught

herself to write in fancy italic writing using silver and gold pens. She even writes notes to my teacher like that to tell her I've got a dental appointment.

Then over the last eighteen months she's got more and more into fairies. She's always been a fairy follower, ever since she was a little girl. I think she actually *believes* in them. She makes weeny fairy furniture, little cotton-reel things with tiny cushions and plaster tables in the shape of toadstools. She sprinkles hundreds and thousands, those tiny rainbow-coloured sweets, on top of the tables. In the morning they're all gone.

'Oh-oh! The fairies had a feast last night!' she says. It's obviously for Robin's benefit, not mine. Though I suppose I used to half believe it when I was his age.

Mum's tried making her own fairies with pipe cleaners and scraps of silk ribbon. She took all the fairy stuff to craft fairs at weekends for a while, but hardly anyone ever bought them. She makes fairy potions too, and special fairy soap with little rosebuds that come off in the bath. Our flat always smells sickly. She buys all the films she can find that have got fairies in them. We have fairy lights all over the flat, even in the toilet.

Robin and I have even got fairy *names*. There's some fairy character called Robin Goodfellow in a play. He's meant to be

very mischievous and plays tricks on people. Our Robin can be mischievous and play tricks, but not in a bad way. He really *is* a good fellow. I'm called Mab. People always think it's short for something, maybe Mabel. No, it's just Mab, after another fairy who was a queen. Still, I suppose it could have been worse. Mum could have chosen another fairy queen – Titania. You can guess what the kids at school would have called me then.

School! Even thinking the word makes my heart start thudding. Home-schooled children are the luckiest kids ever. I hate school. I especially hate Cathy and Anita. They have turned Billie against me. They have a club called the ABCs. The club seems to have only one rule – be as mean and spiteful and mocking as you can to Mab Macclesfield.

I don't mind my teacher. Mrs Horsley's really kind. She's always trying to make lessons fun, and she reads to us at the end of every day and lets us have a dance in the hall when it's a wet lunchtime. She bakes cookies for us and brings in halwa for Diwali, and dresses up at the end of the winter term as Father Christmas – red costume and white beard – and gives us each a little present. She even gives a birthday cupcake to every child when it's their birthday and lets them wear whatever

they like that day, if they want, instead of school uniform, though not everybody does.

Oh no! I thought, *I told Mum this.* I hurriedly dressed in my white blouse and grey skirt before she remembered. I almost got away with it, but when we were going out the door Mum suddenly clapped the palm of her hand to her forehead.

'I've just remembered! You can wear whatever you like today, Mab, because it's your birthday!' she said.

I thought frantically. 'Oh yes, that old rule. But Mrs Horsley's changed her mind. Cathy came to school in a tiny top and shorts a bit like knickers and Mrs Horsley said they were inappropriate, so now none of us are allowed to wear birthday clothes,' I said. I was very proud of myself, especially for using such a grown-up word as *inappropriate*. And Cathy *did* wear that top and shorts, and even the big girls in the top year don't wear clothes like that.

'But Micky in your class wore really cool rapper clothes last week, with sunglasses and a baseball hat!' said Robin. He'd seen him when we went to school and had been very impressed.

'Shut up, Robin!' I muttered, but Mum had heard. It wasn't Robin's fault – he was only trying to be helpful.

He probably thought I was longing to wear my fairy dress to school.

'There you are then, Mab! I'm sure Mrs Horsley wouldn't mind now. And you'll be the envy of all your friends, wearing a *fairy* costume,' said Mum.

I didn't *have* any friends. Perhaps Robin's little friends in Reception might be envious, but my class would fall about laughing.

'There isn't really time to change into my lovely fairy dress now,' I said quickly. 'And I don't want to risk getting it messed up at school. But I'll wear it all day long on Saturday and Sunday.'

The light had gone out of Mum's eyes. I hadn't been convincing enough. 'You don't have to wear it at all, darling, not if you don't like it,' she said.

'I do! I absolutely love it! OK, I'll go and put it on,' I said, unable to help it.

I ran upstairs, pulled off my uniform and wriggled into the fairy dress. Then I took a deep breath and looked in the mirror. It was even worse than I'd thought. It was exactly the right size but still looked totally wrong on me. I don't suit pink for a start. I have pale skin and pink just makes me look plain. I have

plain hair too, long and limp and mousy. I'm bony and I bite my nails. I am so not a fairy sort of girl.

The dress hung on me, the net skirts scratching my legs. It stuck up at the front, because the weight of the wings dragged it down at the back. My scruffy socks and trainers didn't help. I looked a total ninny.

I grabbed a T-shirt and shorts, stuffed them into the pocket of my big raincoat, and ran downstairs.

'Let's see!' said Mum. 'Oh, darling, you look lovely! Look at your new fairy sister, Robin!'

'You're so pretty!' said Robin, clapping his hands.

They weren't teasing – they really meant it. Sometimes I think Mum and Robin come from another planet altogether.

I held my net skirts out and gave them a little twirl, and then quickly pulled on my raincoat.

'I don't think it's going to rain today,' said Mum doubtfully.

'I know. But I want to keep covered up on the way to school so then I can give everyone a surprise when I take it off in the cloakroom,' I said.

'Oh, I get you now,' said Mum. 'Good thinking!'

So we set off schoolwards on my birthday morning, Mum in her maroon shop overall, Robin in his tiny school uniform, and me bundled up in my raincoat, still with at least ten centimetres of shocking pink net showing below the hem.

CHAPTER TWO

We walked to school, Mum and Robin and me. Robin insisted on grabbing our hands and swinging himself backwards and forwards, while singing 'Happy Birthday' to me over and over again. Naturally, people stared, especially at me, the girl wearing a raincoat on a bright sunny day with weird pink netting poking out underneath. Still, there were hardly any other mums and kids about. We always arrived early so that Mum could drop us off by twenty past eight, in time for her shift at the supermarket.

There were a cluster of little Breakfast Club kids at the gate to the Infants, but they didn't bother to give me a

second glance. Several waved at Robin and one small girl actually ran up to him and gave him a smacking kiss on his cheek.

'Robin! Robin! Robin!' she yelled enthusiastically, as if she hadn't seen him for months. She grinned at him. 'He's my boyfriend,' she told her mum proudly.

'No, he's *my* boyfriend,' said a tiny red-haired boy, glaring.

'I can be your boyfriend *and* your boyfriend,' said Robin. 'Bye, Mum. Bye, Mab. Happy Birthday!'

He let go of our hands, grabbed two of his friends' hands instead, and ran into school with them.

'Bless!' said Mum. She turned to me. 'Have a lovely day, darling. Here, birthday treat!' She handed me a chocolate bar.

'Oh, Mum!'

'Shove it in your pocket quick before anyone sees!' said Mum.

Our school is very keen on healthy eating, and the children who take packed lunches are inspected by the Food Police dinner ladies every day. (I have school lunches because I get them free, as Mum doesn't have much money.) It was seriously against the rules to smuggle chocolate into school, but I was good at finding a quiet corner by myself.

'I love you, Mum,' I said, hugging her.

'I love you too, darling,' she said. 'And it'll be birthday tea this afternoon. With a birthday cake. Promise. Are you sure you don't want to invite any of your friends?'

She kept up this myth that I was as popular as my little brother even though she *knew* I wasn't, and *I* knew I wasn't, and she knew I knew. I gave her a big kiss.

'Thank you for my lovely fairy dress,' I said.

'You look a real little Queen Mab,' Mum said. 'Have a great day, darling.'

I skipped across the playground because I knew she was watching me, and then scooted into school, making a beeline for the cloakrooms. Micky (rapper boy, but in ordinary school uniform today) was swinging acrobatically along the coat hooks.

'You'll catch it if a teacher comes past,' I said.

'As if I care,' said Micky. At least the boys in my class still talked to me. The girls were all under Cathy's influence and ignored me completely, apart from holding their noses. At that precise moment the coat hook he was currently holding came right out of the plaster wall. Micky ended up on his bottom, gazing at the hook in his hand in surprise.

He said a very rude word. Then he looked up and saw the white plastery hole in the dark green wall. He said another even ruder word and looked at me.

'Are you going to tell on me?' he demanded.

'Of course not,' I said. 'I'm not a snitch.'

'Yeah, right,' he said challengingly, but he knew I wouldn't. He stood up shakily and felt the small of his back. 'Doesn't half hurt,' he said.

'Rub it,' I suggested.

He tried.

'Does that help?' I asked.

'Not really,' he said.

'Perhaps you should go and see Mrs Black?' I suggested. Mrs Black was the school secretary. She had a first aid certificate so you went to her if you had a headache or felt sick or had a nosebleed.

'Nah, can't be bothered,' said Micky. He was still looking at me. 'What's that you're wearing?'

'A raincoat,' I said, my heart thudding.

'Not the coat thing. What have you got on underneath? The pink stuff?' He pointed at the net of my fairy dress.

'Oh, *that*?' I said. 'It's my ballet frock. I go to ballet classes and I'm in this show and we had an early rehearsal because we're doing the show this Saturday. I get to do a solo dance, with lots of those twirly around things. Pirouettes.'

'Yuck,' said Micky, screwing up his face, but he obviously believed me. I was clearly a gold-star liar.

'You'd be good at ballet,' I said.

'*What?* Catch me prancing around in pink!' said Micky.

'You don't have to wear pink. And boys don't prance. They leap about all over the place,' I said.

Mum and Robin and I had watched a ballet called

The Nutcracker on the telly last Christmas. Mum loved it because of the Sugar Plum Fairy. Robin quite liked it too, though he fell asleep on Mum's lap. I got a bit fidgety, but I liked the rats. I desperately wanted a white rat for a pet. It would look so cool to carry it on my shoulder with its tail hanging down my back like a tiny pink plait. Mum said she loved me very much and maybe one day, when we had a bigger flat and pets would be allowed. She said I could have a cat or even a dog, but she'd never allow me to have a rat of any colour for a pet. For some strange reason Mum is frightened of rats.

'Anyway, I'd better change,' I said, heading for the girls' toilets. I even did a little twirl just to show him.

Then I rushed into a cubicle, took off my raincoat, yanked the terrible fairy dress over my head, and pulled on my shorts and T-shirt. They were my favourite red shorts and the T-shirt was blue with a skateboard on it. At last I felt like myself again.

The fairy dress was too big and bouncy with all its net petticoats to stuff into my bag, but I hid it carefully under my raincoat and hung it in a corner of the cloakroom. I felt almost light-hearted as I sauntered down the corridor into the classroom. That was a mistake. Billie was there, earlier than usual, reading a book.

When she was my best friend instead of my worst enemy, we hung out together all the time. We skipped and ran races at playtime and made up this game where we were circus performers. We both rode white horses and trained dogs to do incredible tricks and walked imaginary tightropes. I suppose it sounds a bit babyish, but we imagined it so intensely that it seemed real. Billie was like me – she *loved* acting out stories.

But then Cathy asked Billie for a sleepover party and she didn't ask me. And then Billie had a sleepover and *she* didn't ask me, even though I was still her best friend. And Anita had a sleepover too and gave them both bangles as special going-home presents. Then they were a trio, and I was on my own.

I asked Billie why she'd gone off me and she said it was my own fault because I never had sleepovers. I didn't even invite her home and yet I'd been to hers for tea three times. Which was true. But I couldn't invite anyone home because our flat smelled a bit of damp and had mould on the ceiling, even though Mum scrubbed at it. She always sprayed everywhere with air freshener and that smelled a bit weird too. Our flat *looked* weird anyway, with all the twinkly lights and the little fairy ornaments on the windowsill and the fairy houses made out of cardboard boxes full of Mum's fairy furniture.

Then Anita and Billie and Cathy noticed that their names went ABC so they started their club, and Cathy said I couldn't be in it because my name didn't start with D. Cathy was the *worst* worst enemy. She said I smelled funny. I was clean as clean and always had a proper stripped-down wash (the shower wouldn't work any more) and my clothes were always clean too, but maybe they did smell a little bit musty because of the damp and the air freshener and the rosewater fairy potions. Anita and Billie and Cathy held their noses now whenever they walked past me, and the other girls copied them. I stuck my chin up and pretended I didn't notice.

I looked at Billie now in the classroom, wondering if she'd hold her nose. She didn't move, head bent over her book, but I could tell she knew I was there. I went to my desk and got out my own school library book. It was an old book, *Catwings*, about these street cats that can fly. It was one of my favourites and I always loved reading it, but I couldn't concentrate on the story right now.

The classroom was eerily quiet. I could hear the sound of my own breathing. I swallowed.

'This is ever such a good book,' I said, glancing at Billie.

For a moment I thought she wasn't going to answer. But

then she made an odd little sound. 'Mm.' Just like that. She still didn't look up though.

'So what are you reading?' I asked.

She hesitated again, and then said, 'It's a book about kittens.'

'No! *My* book's about kittens too! They live in a dustbin but they can fly. It's wicked!' I said. 'What do the kittens do in your story?'

'It's not a story from the library corner. It's my own book from home. Photos of cute kittens. You know, like on YouTube,' she said.

'Can I see?' I said.

Billie shrugged. I took that as an invitation. I went over to her desk and had a good peer at the kittens. They really were cute and I went *oh!* at lots of them.

'I wish I had a kitten!' We *both* said it, together, and then laughed.

Billie looked at me properly then. 'You're wearing your shorts!' she said.

'So?' I said.

'Oh, it's your birthday!' said Billie. She bit her lip, looking awkward. We'd just become friends before my last birthday, and she gave me a big card saying *To my best friend* and a purse

in the shape of a ladybird. I loved that purse, but the zip broke round about the time Billie stopped being my friend.

She was remembering too. 'I'm sorry I haven't got you anything,' she mumbled.

'It's OK,' I said, though it wasn't.

'Well, happy birthday,' she said.

'Thank you.'

'Did you get some nice presents?' Billie asked.

'Yes, terrific,' I said. Robin had given me a little teddy with a goofy face. Mum had obviously paid for it, but he'd chosen it himself. Mrs Watson in the flat underneath us had given me a set of hankies in a box. I think she must have had it in a chest of drawers for donkey's years, but at least she hadn't used them. Michael and Lee in the garden flat had given me a present too, a cactus in a blue bowl. I liked it especially because they'd put a little toy cowboy on a horse riding across the bowl.

I didn't get anything from my dad.

'What did your mum give you?' Billie asked.

I took a deep breath. 'A dress. It's lovely,' I said.

'You don't like dresses much though, do you?' said Billie. 'What sort of dress is it?'

'Oh, a dressy type dress. You know,' I said vaguely. 'And

we're going on a girls night out, to this massive rock concert, and she's got special tickets so I can go backstage for a meet-and-greet, and she's arranged for me to have this ginormous birthday cake and they're going to sing "Happy Birthday" to me . . .'

I was running out of steam and it was clear from Billie's face that she didn't believe a word of it.

'Liar!' she said, but kind of fondly.

'Yeah, well,' I said. 'I got a bit carried away, didn't I?'

'You!' said Billie, and she grinned at me the way she used to.

But then the door opened and some other kids came in. Cathy and Anita weren't with them, but Billie turned her back on me and picked up her book again. When they came skipping into the classroom a few minutes later they did their ABC clapping game – one of their silly club rituals – and all three huddled together, whispering. It was probably about me, because they all looked in my direction and then cracked up laughing. I think they were making rude remarks about my T-shirt and shorts. I was so so so glad the fairy dress was hidden underneath my raincoat.

Mrs Horsley actually admired my outfit, saying she liked the picture of the skateboard on my blue T-shirt and thought

the red shorts very dashing. She was extra nice to me in lessons, and when the bell went for break time she popped a little waxed paper bag on my desk.

'Happy birthday!' she said, smiling. 'Don't let the dinner ladies see!'

It was a birthday cupcake with blue buttercream icing studded with silver balls and blueberries. I sauntered over behind the bike sheds and ate both my birthday treats, taking alternate bites of cake and chocolate. They were delicious, though I felt a bit queasy afterwards and didn't feel very hungry when it was lunchtime. I went back to my secret corner and read *Catwings*. Because no one could see me behind the bike sheds I sucked my thumb too, which was very comforting.

We had art in the afternoon. Mrs Horsley showed us pictures by famous artists like Constable and Van Gogh and asked us all to paint a landscape. I did one of my jungle paintings, with a gorilla thumping his chest and elephants trumpeting and a stripy tiger creeping through the undergrowth, looking sinister. I coiled a green and yellow snake round a tree, with its forked tongue sticking out, ready to attack.

'Um, Smelly's doing it all wrong,' said Cathy, peering over at my picture. 'We're meant to be painting countryside.'

'Trust her to be stupid,' said Anita.

'But doesn't a jungle count as countryside?' said Billie.

'Of course it doesn't!' said Cathy. 'Are you sticking up for old Smelly?'

'No, I was just saying,' said Billie, but she glanced over at me apologetically.

The ABC club watched as Mrs Horsley circled the room, looking at everyone's paintings. They nudged each other as she approached me.

'Oh, Mab, that's an amazing painting!' she said. 'Well, I'm definitely going to pin that one up on the wall. Well done! I love that snake sticking out its tongue!'

When she moved on to the next table, I stuck my own tongue out at Anita and Cathy. Not Billie. She might still be a little bit friends with me.

Then it was going-home time. It would have been very difficult trying to change back into the fairy dress without the ABC club seeing me, but luckily Robin and I never went home straight away. We went to After School Club until five o'clock, when Mum collected us after her shift at the supermarket. The only other person in my class who went to After School Club was Micky, and I'd already convinced him it was a ballet dress.

I waited a few minutes to let the other kids go charging off home and then went to the toilets to scrub my green hands. Some of my jungle seemed to have rubbed off on me. I stopped short when I got to the cloakroom. Anita and Billie and Cathy were still there, taking it in turns to try on Cathy's cool new backpack. They were also pointing at my raincoat.

'It must come down to Smelly's ankles!' said Cathy.

'And why is she wearing it to school anyway? It's boiling hot,' said Anita.

'I'm going to try it on!' said Cathy, running up to it.

'Don't you dare!' I yelled.

'She's only teasing, Mab,' Billie said quickly. 'You know we're not allowed to wear each other's clothes.'

'*I'm* allowed!' said Cathy, starting to pull it off the coat hook. 'Phew, it stinks!'

'Shut *up*!' I shouted.

But all three of them were suddenly silent as the pink fairy frock fell out of my raincoat. The limp wings flapped weakly as it tumbled to the floor.

'What on earth is *that*?' said Anita.

'It's a *fairy frock*!' Cathy shrieked, beside herself.

'No it's not. It's for my ballet class,' I said.

'But you don't do ballet,' said Billie. I think she was just bewildered, but it sounded like she was joining in.

'Oh, this is priceless! An actual fairy frock! Oh, lickle Mab, does yoo skip awound playing fairwies?' Cathy went on relentlessly.

'Shut up, shut up, shut up!' I said, trying to pull the dress away from her.

She pulled too and there was a sudden rip.

'You beast! You've torn it deliberately!' I cried, snatching it away from her. 'It's a present from my mum!'

I pictured Mum's face crumpling. I was so angry I ran at Cathy and pushed her. It wasn't the hardest push in the world and Cathy's bigger than me, but I took her off guard. She slipped. She screamed as she staggered back, then landed in a heap on the floor.

'My ankle! Oh, my ankle – it *hurts*! It's total agony! I'm sure you've broken it, Mab Macclesfield! You're going to get in so much trouble!' she yelled.

CHAPTER THREE

I stared at her, horrified. I hadn't meant to hurt her. I'd only wanted to push her away. And I didn't see how one little stumble could really break her ankle. But what if she had really broken it? She'd have to go to hospital and they'd ask her how she'd done it. She'd say *I'd* done it. Maybe the doctor might call the police! Or even if she just told a teacher, I was still in serious trouble, because our school has a strict no-fighting policy. Maybe I'd be *suspended*?

'Girls, girls, what's this awful noise?'

Mrs Horsley was hurrying down the corridor towards us, her shoes squeaking on the polished floor. Even Mrs Horsley

would stop liking me! This was such a terrible thought that I burst into tears.

'Oh dear, what's the matter, Mab?' Mrs Horsley said.

'It's not her that's hurt, miss, it's me!' said Cathy indignantly from the floor. 'I've broken my ankle! And *she* did it! She pushed me right over, didn't she?' She looked at Anita and Billie for support. They shuffled a bit, embarrassed. Everyone in our class had a rule that we never ever told on anyone, not to a teacher.

'Now then!' said Mrs Horsley, getting down on her knees beside her with a little difficulty. Mrs Horsley is quite a large lady. 'Which ankle is it, Cathy?'

'This one!' said Cathy, sticking her leg out.

Mrs Horsley looked at it carefully, and gently twisted it this way and that. 'Well, it's definitely not broken,' she said.

'Then maybe it's this one,' said Cathy, waggling her other leg.

Mrs Horsley examined that one too. 'Do you know something, Cathy?' she said, hauling herself up with a lot more difficulty. 'I think your ankles are absolutely fine.'

I gave a little snort of relief. It might have sounded like a giggle. Cathy flashed me a look of hatred.

Mrs Horsley sighed. Then she looked at me properly and saw I was clutching something violently pink. 'What have you got there, Mab?' she asked.

'It's her fairy dress, miss,' said Anita. The three of them really did giggle then. Even Billie.

'Let me see,' said Mrs Horsley.

I held it out speechlessly. The dress hung limply, net skirts ruffled, the wings hanging lopsidedly.

'Oh dear,' said Mrs Horsley. She examined them carefully. 'How did it get torn?' she asked.

Silence. Cathy was looking at me fearfully now. But I decided not to tell. Anyway, Mrs Horsley looked as if she'd

guessed how it happened. She shook her head sadly.

'Oh, girls! Why can't you all be friends?' she asked, but she didn't seem to expect an answer to that either. 'Well, run along, Anita, Billie and Cathy. Your parents will be wondering where you've got to.'

They ran. Well, Cathy hobbled, but I'm sure she was just pretending her leg was hurting. Mrs Horsley seemed to think so too, but she said, 'Cathy, go in to see Mrs Black first. She'll have a look at that ankle too – if you can remember which one it is.'

Then she looked at me.

'It's a very pretty fairy dress,' she said softly. She seemed to think it was my choice. I wanted to tell her I thought it was hideous, but I couldn't be disloyal to Mum.

'Thank you,' I murmured, sniffling. 'But it's torn now.'

'It's actually only a little rip,' said Mrs Horsley comfortingly. 'I'll take it with me into the staffroom and see if I can mend it. I'll bring it to you at the After School Club, all right?'

I nodded.

'Is it your birthday present?' she asked.

I nodded again.

'It's very special,' said Mrs Horsley. 'Do you know

something? When I was a little girl *I* had a fairy dress. I absolutely loved it.'

I was amazed. It was certainly very hard imagining a young Mrs Horsley dancing around in a fairy dress.

I felt faintly cheered going to After School Club. Robin was sitting with Micky, both of them drawing something, but they covered the paper up when they saw me. Robin ran over and greeted me as if we hadn't seen each other for months.

'What are you drawing with Micky?' I asked suspiciously. 'It's not anything rude, is it?'

'No!' said Robin, giggling.

'Then why are you hiding it?' I asked.

'Because it's a secret,' said Robin. 'Where've you been?'

I shrugged. 'Just talking to my teacher,' I said.

My eyes must have still been watery because Robin looked anxious. 'Was she telling you off?' he asked.

'Don't worry. Mrs Horsley's always having a go at me too,' said Micky, truthfully enough. He was always in trouble for talking or losing his notebook or pencils, or for generally messing about. 'But she's not a bad old stick really,' he added.

'I like her,' I said. 'She's mending my . . . ballet dress for me at the moment.'

Robin blinked at the word *ballet*, but I shot him my *do-not-say-a-word!* look, and he managed to hold it in.

'Did it get torn then?' Micky asked.

'Just a bit,' I said.

'It was that ABC club, wasn't it?' said Micky. He can act dim sometimes but he's good at sussing things out.

I didn't say anything, but it was obvious he was right.

'I'll sort them out for you,' said Micky. He spoke out of the side of his mouth, pretending to be a gangster. 'You leave it to me!'

'Thanks but no thanks!' I said, sitting down at the table beside them. 'I'll do a bit of drawing too. Only I haven't got any unlined paper. Or felt pens.' I looked enviously at Micky's. It was exactly the sort of colouring set I'd have loved as a birthday present – and it would probably have cost much less than my fairy dress.

I wondered if Mrs Horsley could really mend it so that it was as good as new. I hoped she wouldn't tell anyone else in the staffroom what had happened. I didn't want them feeling sorry for me.

It was calm and peaceful in the After School Club. Micky tore a page out of his drawing book for me and let me

share his felt tips too. He hid his own drawing, putting his arm round the page and leaning forward, totally blocking my view. Robin tried to do the same, but he wasn't as good at it. I glimpsed the word *Robin* at the bottom of his page, with two rows of kisses, and felt a little glow. I was pretty sure he was making me a birthday card. I had no idea what Micky was doing. Perhaps *he* was drawing a rude picture.

We had snack time – a small cup of milk and a biscuit out of a big tin. You weren't supposed to choose. You had to dip your hand in and take whatever your fingers touched, but we were all clever at feeling. Why would you take a boring old digestive when you could feel the shiny paper of a chocolate biscuit?

Mrs Horsley came into the room at quarter past four. She was carrying a supermarket bag for life with something bulky inside. My fairy dress. I peeped at it. She'd smoothed out the net skirts and reattached the wings, so that they flapped perkily now. It was still hideous, but at least it was as good as new. And she'd had the tact to put the dress in a bag so that no one could see it and mock.

'Thank you so so so much, Mrs Horsley!' I said. I would

have liked to have hugged her, but I wasn't sure you were allowed to do that to a teacher.

There was something else under the fairy dress, weighing the bag down. I delved in for it, puzzled. It was a big school library book called *Victorian Fairy Paintings*.

'I thought you might like to look at it,' said Mrs Horsley. 'Nobody's ever borrowed it so I daresay you could keep it if you'd like to.'

'Oh, that's so kind of you!' I said. I didn't want the book for myself as I wasn't the slightest bit interested in fairies, but I knew who was.

'Teacher's pet!' Micky muttered.

'Oh, sorry, Micky, do you feel left out?' said Mrs Horsley. 'Shall I see if I can find a special fairy book for you too?'

Robin laughed so hard at the idea of his great big bad hero Micky wanting a fairy book that he nearly choked on his last bite of biscuit and had to be thumped on his back.

'Happy birthday again!' said Mrs Horsley, smiling at me.

She was like a great big fairy herself. She certainly didn't *look* very fairy-like with her grey hair and glasses and navy dress and sturdy shoes, but it was as if she had a magic wand and always made things better for me.

Robin handed me his piece of paper with a big grin on his face. He had drawn a blob with long hair and stick arms and legs. It was holding hands with a littler blob with a big smile on its face. There was wobbly printing at the top – *Hapy Burthdy* – and *Luv Robin* at the bottom, with all those kisses.

'The big one is you and the little one is me and I'm smiling because I'm so happy you're my sister,' said Robin.

I gave him a big hug though he squirmed a bit, embarrassed in front of Micky.

'Here,' said Micky, and he gave me his piece of paper too. He'd made me a birthday card too! He was quite good at drawing because he read lots of comics and copied the pictures. He'd drawn me wearing my so-called ballet dress, but my net skirts were fanned out because I was riding on a seriously cool electric scooter. He'd written *Happy Birthday* at the top and scrawled *Micky* at the bottom.

'I'm riding a scooter!' I said.

'Maybe you'll get a real one for your birthday next year,' he said.

'Yeah, pigs might fly,' I said, but I was very touched.

When the After School Club closed I had to hurtle to the cloakroom to change into my fairy dress and put my raincoat

on. There was a square sandwich bag on the bench underneath my raincoat. There was a little note too on a torn-out page from a notebook.

Sorry about what happened. This is for you. Happy Birthday. Love from Billie xxx

She'd given me her cute kitten book! *Two* birthday present books and two cards! I held hands with Robin and skipped across the playground to Mum.

'Did you have a good day, darling?' she asked.

'Brilliant,' I said. 'Look, presents! And two cards.'

Mum looked very pleased. She cooed over Robin's card but looked a little doubtfully at Micky's.

'Isn't he the naughty boy who keeps getting into trouble?' she said.

'He's OK,' I said.

'He's wicked!' said Robin.

'I'll say,' said Mum. 'So is one of your presents from Billie?' she added, looking pleased.

'She gave me this kitten book – look!'

Mum seemed thrilled that she'd given me her book, though she was puzzled about the note. 'Why is she saying sorry?' she asked.

'Don't know,' I said, shrugging.

'I guessed you and Billie might have had a few tiffs recently,' said Mum. 'But she hasn't been really nasty to you, has she?'

Robin opened his mouth, but I shot him my special look again, and he knew not to say a word.

'Wait till you see the other birthday present book, Mum,' I said, fishing it out of the bag for life.

'Oh my! Fairies!' said Mum, reading the title. But when she opened it she saw the library form inside. 'But it's a library book, Mab!'

'It's OK. It's a present from Mrs Horsley. She said I could keep it,' I said.

'Really, truly?' said Mum. 'I know you get a bit carried away sometimes, Mab. Maybe you *wanted* her to say that?'

'No, she really really did,' I insisted. 'It's my present. And you can have a share of it, Mum, seeing as you're so into fairies.'

'Can't I have a share in it too? *I* like fairies,' said Robin.

'OK, it's a present for all of us,' I said. 'We'll look at it together when we get home.'

But we didn't look at it for quite a while. First of all there was a letter on the hall floor. We didn't often get letters, only bills and adverts. I picked it up.

Miss M. Macclesfield it said, in purple ink and fancy italic writing.

'Who's this from?' I asked.

'I wonder,' said Mum.

'It's not from Dad, is it?' I said, my heart thumping.

'Maybe!' said Mum. 'Look inside!'

I opened up the envelope. It wasn't a letter – it was a card. It had a picture of a girl on the front, strangely enough in a ballet dress. She had curls and dimples and was raising her arms and pointing her toes in the most graceful fashion.

The silver lettering at the top said *To my Birthday Princess.*

'What a lovely card!' said Mum. 'There, Mab! Dad's remembered your birthday. Is there anything inside?'

There was a twenty-pound note.

'Wow, that's heaps of money!' said Robin.

I'd never had so much money before. Yet I was old enough to know Dad never sent Mum any money for our keep. Twenty pounds didn't seem so much when you compared it with the huge amount he owed Mum. And he never bothered to get in touch properly. He just sent cards at Christmas, often without any money at all. Mum always said Dad was a free spirit and had to go his own way sometimes. He was a musician and everyone knew they were different, she said. When they'd been together, she'd never nagged him.

'Is there a message?' Mum asked.

'Yes,' I said. I read it out loud in a shaky voice:

'To my best girl – I know I haven't seen you much recently but believe me, I think about you all the time. You must be turning into a lovely young lady now. I wonder if you ever think about your old dad? Take care, little sweetheart, and look after your mum and your baby brother for me. Heaps of hugs and birthday kisses, from Dad.'

'Yuck!' I pulled a face.

'Don't, Mab! It's a really lovely message!' said Mum.

'I wish you'd stop saying Dad's *lovely*,' I shouted.

'Hey, hey, you can't get cross on your birthday!' said Mum.

I clamped my lips together. I wanted to be cross. I wanted to shout and scream because it was so unfair of Dad to come weaselling back into our lives when Mum was so much better now and we'd almost stopped missing him. But I could see I was only upsetting Mum and frightening Robin.

Mrs Horsley had taught us to take five deep breaths before we lost our tempers or said something unkind. Nobody took any notice, especially Cathy and Anita, but I tried now to see if it worked. I breathed in slowly slowly slowly and then out in a great whoosh – so my nose made a loud snorty noise. It made Robin giggle and Mum rush for a tissue. And maybe it did work because I calmed down.

'Shall I treat us all to a giant pizza with my birthday money?' I suggested.

'You can't spend it just like that, Mab! You need to buy something really special that will last for ever,' said Mum. 'Something only for you, that will give you great pleasure.'

'I've already got my fairy dress,' I said heroically. 'And if I'm a fairy now, I can grant my own wishes, and so I wish for

the biggest-size pizza with extra cheese and pineapple, and I promise I'll remember this birthday for ever and ever!'

So I put my raincoat back on over my fairy dress and the three of us walked to Pizza Palace and we bought the giant pizza. Mum carried the huge cardboard box home, holding it in front of her like a tray, while Robin and I skipped along either side of her.

I kept my fairy dress on while we ate the pizza at home, though Mum tied a tea towel round my neck just in case I spilled any. I leaned forward on my chair so I wouldn't crush my wings. Now that Mrs Horsley had sewn them both more tightly so they weren't so limp they almost seemed to have a life of their own, waving up and down at my slightest movement. I found them very unnerving.

Robin ate two big slices of pizza and Mum and I shared the rest between us. It was utterly delicious. I think I could have eaten the entire pizza by myself actually. But it was good I didn't as I still had room for my birthday cake. It was the supermarket special – a round sponge with jam and cream in the middle and a lot of pink icing, with three pink sugary roses on the top. I'd have preferred the other birthday cake they did, a red train with black wheels in a Swiss roll shape, but I knew

we'd probably have that one when it was Robin's birthday.

Mum stuck candles carefully round the roses and lit them. 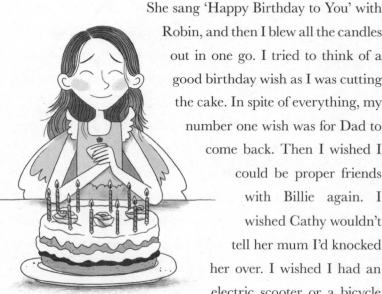 She sang 'Happy Birthday to You' with Robin, and then I blew all the candles out in one go. I tried to think of a good birthday wish as I was cutting the cake. In spite of everything, my number one wish was for Dad to come back. Then I wished I could be proper friends with Billie again. I wished Cathy wouldn't tell her mum I'd knocked her over. I wished I had an electric scooter or a bicycle or a giant colouring set.

I wished I *didn't* have a fairy dress. I wished all the little tinkly fairy ornaments in our flat would spread their tiny wings and flap out of the window.

CHAPTER FOUR

Mum suggested we play party games after tea. There weren't really enough of us but it didn't matter as we were only fooling around. We played musical statues, Robin and me dancing about until Mum suddenly switched the radio off. Then we had to stand completely still, not moving. Robin was hopeless at it, wobbling all over the place, so I won every time. Then we played hunt the thimble. We used a little china thimble ornament painted with weeny fairies. Mum was quite good at hiding it and so was I. Robin hid the thimble in his pocket and we tried to explain to him that the thimble had to be in plain sight. Next time he put the thimble on his nose and

looked so funny that we fell about laughing.

We tried blind man's bluff, covering my eyes with a scarf
so I had to blunder around the living room until I found Mum
and Robin. It was easy-peasy finding Robin because I could
hear him breathing excitedly. The game became chaotic when
Robin wore the scarf because he charged about wildly, flinging
his arms around, and knocked a flock of fairies off the coffee
table. They were the little metal kind so they didn't break, but
Mum decided to call a halt to the party games.

'Let's sit on the sofa together and look at Mab's lovely fairy
book,' she suggested.

She sat down with the book on her lap. Robin one side of
her and I on the other. There was a portrait of a fairy on the
front cover with blue eyes and rosy cheeks and a little red
mouth. She had long curly golden hair kept in place with
brightly coloured butterflies, like a living Alice band. She
looked a little bit like Cathy.

'She's so lovely!' Mum sighed, stroking her curls.

'Beautiful!' Robin agreed.

I flicked her neat little nose with my thumb and forefinger.
Mum started turning the glossy pages.

'Goodness!' she said, coming to a picture of fairies dancing.

They weren't the usual child fairies skipping about daintily. They were adults, and very skimpily dressed. The ladies didn't have any tops on and several men were stark naked.

'Boobies! Bottoms!' said Robin, giggling.

Mum tutted and turned the page. There were more grown-up fairies, wearing even less. They all looked very fierce, and were brandishing sticks, beating at a big spider.

'Ugh!' said Mum and turned the page again. She has a thing about spiders. She always cowers away from even tiny ones.

The next picture was quite hard to puzzle out. It was very dark, and you had to peer through great strands of grass to see what was going on. There were a lot of fairy folk standing around amongst some daisies, but some were big and some were small and all of them looked very weird.

Robin peered at them, his nose very close to the page.

'Are they fairies?' he asked, puzzled. 'The ladies don't look pretty at all. They're all pointy and their legs are a funny shape and they're all standing on top of each other.'

'There's no top or bottom to the picture,' I said. 'You can't work out where they all are.'

'I don't like that little fairy man!' said Robin, suddenly

rearing back. 'He looks like he's going to come right out of the page and get me.'

'It's doing my head in,' said Mum, and she closed the book quickly. 'It was very kind of Mrs Horsley to give it to you, Mab, but it's not suitable for children. They're not lovely fairies who are kind and good and make magic spells. The ones in this big book are horrid. Let's read about some nice fairies instead.'

She got out her precious set of Flower Fairies books she'd had since she was a little girl. She didn't let us borrow them in case we tore a page or left sticky fingerprints. She only read them to us for special treats. Robin loves them. I used to like them too, when I was very little, but I think they're a bit sickly now.

I rather *liked* the fairies in Mrs Horsley's book. They made me wonder if fairies were actually rather interesting after all. Not all tinkly and pretty and pink.

When I woke up in the middle of the night I climbed quietly out of bed and crept across the room in the dark, trying hard not to bump into anything. It's quite hard because my bedroom's very small, not much bigger than a cupboard. Mum and Robin sleep in the big bedroom. I love having my own room. Mum wanted to paint it pink to make it a special girly

room for me. I begged her to let me choose my own colour scheme. It's painted deep green and I have a big fluffy green rug on the floor. I've dangled a toy snake from the ceiling, and the big tiger I won at a fair crouches in the corner. It's like my own tiny jungle.

I crept into the living room, felt for the fairy book on the sofa, and found the torch in the kitchen drawer. Mum keeps it there in case of power cuts. Then I scurried back to bed, switched on the torch and opened the book.

The fairies looked quite scary in the torchlight. I flipped past the weird adult fairies and the spider and found a painting of a man fast asleep, with strange ghostly fairies capering all around him. He had thick golden hair and a beard. I suppose he looked a little like my dad. Robin's got that lovely golden hair too. It's not fair that my hair's plain mouse. The painting was called *The Painter's Dream* – and then there was page after page of the fairy pictures. There were fairies having a banquet; gliding along a stream in a water lily; fighting a bat; curling up in a bird's nest; nursing a squirrel and a fawn; riding a rabbit; and huddling together with a woolly sheep in the snow. He'd even painted a fairy funeral with pale sad fairies mourning a limp white one on a leafy bed, her long hair trailing.

I pored over it for a long time and then turned the page. A little soft flat thing fell onto my lap. It looked like a pressed flower. Mum had bought a flower-pressing kit at a boot fair once and had enjoyed this new hobby. She couldn't carry on for long though because we couldn't afford to buy flowers all the time. There weren't any in the small garden at the back of our house – it was just gravel with two matching palms in pots – and we couldn't grow any flowers there because it didn't belong to us. Michael and Lee had the garden flat, and they said we could play in the garden any time, but Mum didn't like to take advantage.

I picked up the pressed flower very carefully. It was white, but much bigger than a daisy. Perhaps it was a lily of some sort. I held it to my nose but it didn't have the faintest smell.

I peered at it closely. *Was* it a flower? I couldn't quite make it out. I held it for a long time on the palm of my hand, looking at it this way and that. It was a shame it was so crushed and papery so I popped it in my water glass to see if it might plump up a bit, and then I huddled down and went to sleep.

I dreamed of fairies then. Strange creatures, distorted, some shining so brightly they made me blink, others crawling along in the shadows with snail horns and slime trails that made me shudder. I must have tossed and turned a lot in my sleep because my duvet was on the floor when I woke up.

I sat up in my tumbled bed, rubbing my eyes and yawning. My mouth was dry so I reached for my water glass, took a sip – and got a mouthful of pressed flower. I spat it back into the glass and stared. It seemed bigger, and it had uncurled in the night. The petals stuck out now, two spread out almost as if they were wings. And then one fluttered.

I stared at it. How could it have moved? It was a long-dead flower. Had I nudged the

glass and caused a little wave? I put my finger in the water and stirred it like a teaspoon. The flower bobbed up and down a little, but that was all. I'd been imagining things.

I looked at my old clock. It was a fairy one, of course, with chubby-cheeked baby fairies sitting on a toadstool. The big and little hands of the clock (fairy wands!) were pointing accusingly at the time. Five to eight!

'Mum! Robin! Get up – we've overslept!' I cried, leaping out of bed and rushing to the big bedroom.

'Oh, dear goodness, I forgot to set my alarm,' said Mum, sitting bolt upright. She put her hand over her mouth. 'What's the matter with me?'

'Perhaps those fairies in the book cast a spell on you because you said they were horrid,' I said, trying to tickle Robin out of bed. It was just a silly joke to stop her feeling upset, but she looked stricken.

'You don't really think that, do you?' she whispered.

'*Mum!*' I said. 'They're only *pictures* of weird fairies. They're not *real*.'

'Of course I don't think they're real,' said Mum, though she didn't sound utterly convinced. She always said she surrounded us with little fairy pictures and fairy ornaments

and children's fairy stories to make us feel safe and happy, so I suppose strange creepy fairies might make her feel frightened.

'Don't look so anxious, Mum!' I said.

'Of course I'm anxious – I'm going to be late for work!' said Mum, dashing to the bathroom. 'Can you start getting breakfast ready, Mab?'

I breathed a sigh of relief. She was ordinary Mum again, fussing about being late. I made tea and prepared us all honey sandwiches. We had a lick-and-a-promise wash and pulled on our clothes. Robin put his school shirt on back to front and his shoes on the wrong feet, but he was only trying to be helpful. We gulped down our drinks and then ate the sandwiches as we hurried down the road.

Robin was very sticky by the time we got to school so Mum had to spit on a tissue and wipe his hands and mouth as best she could. He went skipping into school, Mum went scurrying off to the supermarket, and I trudged across the playground. Mrs Horsley was just arriving, her arms full of notebooks and flowers from her garden and a Tupperware box with a cupcake for some other birthday child.

'Shall I help you carry something, Mrs Horsley?' I offered.

'Perhaps the roses?' she suggested. 'Though mind you

don't scratch yourself on any thorns. Bless you, Mab. If I believed in gold stars I'd stick one right in the middle of your forehead.'

'I found a pressed flower inside the pages of the fairy book you gave me,' I said. 'Did you put it there?'

'No, pet, I didn't. I bought a whole pile of books from the church fete years ago, thinking they'd liven up the school library, but I haven't got a clue who'd donated them. How did you get on with the book? I was actually having second thoughts about it last night. It might have taken you by surprise. Those Victorian painters were an odd bunch,' she said.

'I like it ever so much,' I said enthusiastically. 'I spent ages looking at the pictures.'

'Well, that's good,' said Mrs Horsley, smiling, as we went into school together. 'Now, I think I can battle my way to the staffroom without further help. How about you take the roses to the classroom and put them in a vase for me?'

'OK,' I said, pleased.

'In the old days I always used to choose a child to be my flower monitor,' she said.

'I'd love to be your flower monitor, Mrs Horsley.'

'Consider yourself appointed!' she said. 'See you later then.'

I carried the roses carefully, clasping them with two hands. Micky was seeing if he could jump the short distance between the benches in the cloakrooms. It wasn't short enough and he landed on his bottom again.

'Ouch,' I said sympathetically. 'And you've probably already got a great big bruise from larking about yesterday.'

'Yeah, it's a massive dark purple one,' said Micky. 'And now it will get even purpler.'

'Well, so long as it doesn't go bright red, because then you'll look as if you're turning into a baboon,' I said.

Micky spluttered with laughter, not at all offended. 'What are you carrying them flowers for, Mab?' he asked.

'Mrs Horsley gave me them because I just happen to be her new flower monitor,' I said.

'Get you. I said you were a teacher's pet,' said Micky. He looked me up and down. 'So, no ballet lesson today?'

'Nope.'

'I still think ballet's daft anyway. All silly and fancy.' Micky pranced about in a ridiculous fashion.

'You're the one who's daft,' I said.

We weren't really quarrelling. It was only banter. I left him practising his death-defying leaps and went into the classroom.

I very much hoped Billie would be there early so I could thank her for the kitten book. But she wasn't.

I spent a long time arranging the roses, trying to get them into a perfect circle, and then put them on Mrs Horsley's desk. They were the lovely crimson kind that smelled beautiful.

Billie didn't come into the classroom until the bell rang, and she had Anita on one side and Cathy on the other. I tried to catch her eye so I could mouth *thank you* at her, but she was determinedly looking the other way. Cathy came right up to me though. She was wearing a big white bandage on her left leg and was limping in an exaggerated manner.

'I've got a very bad sprained ankle because of you,' she said. 'My mum and dad are furious. Dad wanted to come to school to complain, but Mum talked him out of it. She says maybe you're disturbed because your mum's a bit doolally.'

I could feel myself going as red as Mrs Horsley's roses. 'How dare you! My mum is *not* doolally!' I'd never even heard that horrible expression before, but I knew what she meant. 'There's absolutely nothing wrong with my mum. And I hardly even touched you yesterday. I bet your ankle isn't sprained at all. You're just determined to make a great big fuss. You only want to get me into trouble!'

I was shouting at the top of my voice just as Mrs Horsley walked into the classroom.

'What on earth is going on!' she said. 'Who's doing all that shouting?'

There was a sudden silence. Cathy looked at me, her lips clamped shut showing that *she* wasn't shouting. Her eyes were gleaming. Everyone else was looking at me too. It was obvious that *I* was the culprit.

'Well, pipe down, whoever it was. *I'm* the only person allowed to shout in this classroom,' said Mrs Horsley. 'Now, let's start our day together sensibly. Good morning, children!'

'Good morn-ing Mis-sis Hors-ley,' everyone chanted.

'That's better. Whenever anyone feels cross again, come and smell these beautiful roses fresh from my garden. Mmm!' she said, bending over the vase and breathing in their scent. 'I defy anyone to come up with a lovelier smell.'

'What about fish and chips, miss?' said Micky, and everyone laughed.

'I *said* you were teacher's pet,' he muttered to me later. 'Mrs Horsley knew it was you and yet she didn't tell you off. Don't blame you for shouting at that Cathy though. You sure you don't want me to beat her up?'

'I'll beat her up myself if she dares say another word about my mum,' I said fiercely.

'Don't know what she's going on about. Your mum's lovely. She's always all smiley when she sees you,' said Micky.

'Yes, she is, isn't she?' I said. I tried to think of something nice I could say about Micky's mum. She was quite old and had very short grey hair and wore a thick aqua cardigan even if it was boiling hot. 'I like your mum's cardigan,' I said lamely.

'That's not my *mum*!' said Micky. 'That's my nan. She looks after me and Joey now my mum's not around.'

'Oh, Micky!' I lowered my voice to a whisper. 'Did your mum die?'

'Nah. She just went off,' he said. He shrugged in a couldn't-care-less sort of way but I wasn't fooled.

'Well, my dad went off,' I said. I hadn't told anyone at school before, except Billie. And now Cathy and Anita probably knew too.

'Ah,' said Micky. He nodded at me. I nodded back at him.

At lunchtime Micky played football with a gang of other boys – but after about ten minutes he came wandering over to the bike sheds. He had somehow purloined the football and was trying to do keepy-uppies.

'Hi, you!' he said, and the ball bounced over to the bikes.

'Hi,' I said.

'That's my brother's mountain bike, the flash one. I'd let you have a short ride on it, but my brother would kill me. He won't even let me ride it,' said Micky, retrieving the ball and starting again.

'It's OK,' I said.

'I wish he was my *little* brother. Then *I'd* have the bike and he'd be the one thinking it's not fair. Plus he might be a bit like your brother. He's a great kid, isn't he?' The ball bounced away from him.

'Yes, he is,' I said as he went to get it.

'And if he was my little brother then you'd be my sister, and no one would ever dare be mean to you,' said Micky. He only managed two kicks this time. 'Funny, I'm usually great at keepy-uppies. Maybe it's because I'm talking to you,' he said. 'Still, I've got to practise. I'm working on the world record.

My brother says he did twenty-seven once, but nobody was watching and he tells lies sometimes.'

'So do I. Sort of. My mum says it doesn't matter if they're kind lies. Like if I was to say you're absolutely great at keepy-uppies then it would be a kind lie, wouldn't it?' I said.

'Not necessarily. You could be speaking the absolute truth,' said Micky huffily. 'It's way more difficult than it looks, you know.'

'Can I have a go then?'

Micky kicked the ball in my direction. I stood up and gave it a try. I was rubbish the first three times because I'd never done it before. I didn't have a football or a place to practise in.

'If I was telling a kind lie, I'd say *you're* absolutely great at it,' said Micky, grinning in a most irritating manner.

I kept on trying. I managed two the next time, which was still a bit pathetic, though Micky clapped in a patronizing manner. Then I managed four. I'd got the knack! I did four again, then five, then a totally glorious *eight*!

'Now you're rocking!' said Micky. 'Why haven't I got a phone? This needs recording!'

'I'm getting cramp in my leg,' I said. 'Let's play footie together.'

We moved out from behind the bike sheds and started kicking the ball about. I was quite nifty. Better than Micky. I kept hooking the ball away from him. He got annoyed and decided to tackle me. He went charging at the ball like a bull and I went flying.

'Oh, Mab! Are you all right? I didn't mean to knock you over!' he said, looking horrified.

'I'm fine,' I said, picking myself up. 'Though this is football not rugby, and if this was a real game you'd get sent off with a red card.'

'You haven't sprained your ankle, have you?' he asked anxiously.

'Who do you think I am – Cathy Brittany?' I asked.

'Cathy *Brat*-tany, more like,' said Micky. He roared with laughter at his own joke. It wasn't that funny but I laughed too.

Anita and Billie and Cathy were just in front of us when we went back into school for afternoon lessons. Cathy was walking normally – in fact, she was jigging about demonstrating some silly dance routine – but when she saw us she started limping again.

'Oh, poor Cathy, her leg seems really bad,' said Micky in a

loud voice. 'Don't like the look of it at all. I think she should go to hospital and have it put in plaster.'

'And then she'll have to wear one of those big boot things all the time,' I said.

'Well, that's OK, because she's an ugly old boot herself,' said Micky, quick as a flash.

Cathy turned round, her face screwed up in fury. 'Don't you dare mock me, Mab Macclesfield and Micky Flynn! I'm telling!' she said.

'Do you hear the special birdsong of the Greater Spotted Tell-Tale Tit?' said Micky. 'It goes *I'mtelling I'mtelling I'mtelling!*'

This was an even better joke. Micky's football pals heard and they all laughed too. Even Billie and Anita pursed their lips to stop themselves giggling, though they followed Cathy as she rushed into the classroom, going step-shuffle, step-shuffle, step-shuffle. She got mixed up in her fury, and transferred her limp to the leg without the bandage. The boys all noticed this too and laughed more. I felt almost sorry for Cathy, which was the strangest feeling ever.

I was really happy that afternoon. Mrs Horsley announced we were all going to do a special project for the rest of the summer term. She'd even ordered us some special big new

notebooks with lined pages one side and plain pages the other, so we could write about our special subject and then do drawings or stick pictures on the plain pages.

'What *is* the special subject, miss?' Micky asked. 'Can it be football?'

'Can it be dancing, Mrs Horsley?' Anita begged.

'Can it be Fortnite, miss?' said several boys.

'You can each choose your own subject. It could be football. It could be dancing. It could be a video game you love. You can choose anything you're really interested in, but I want you to study it in depth. Go into the history of your subject. Explain why it fascinates you. I want a personal account, not pages copied word for word from the internet. Use the school library and the local library as well as your search engines,' said Mrs Horsley.

'Will there be a prize for the best project, Mrs Horsley?' Cathy asked. She'd won a prize for best homework when we were in Mr Tompkins' class last year, although everyone knew her mum had done it all for her. Perhaps Mrs Horsley knew too.

'I'm not too keen on the idea of prizes, Cathy,' said Mrs Horsley, 'but I'll give it some thought. And I'd like all of

you to mull things over tonight and then tell me tomorrow what your chosen project will be.'

'I bags football,' George Smith said quickly. He's already in the school football team and a bit of a show-off.

Half the class complained loudly.

'You don't have to reserve a subject. I don't mind if several people choose the same one. As long as each project is individual,' said Mrs Horsley.

'We're in a club together, so we'll each do different sorts of dancing,' Cathy announced.

Anita nodded enthusiastically. Billie nodded too but looked disappointed. She wasn't really keen on dancing. She probably wanted to do a project on a topic she'd chosen herself.

When the bell went Cathy made for the door, expecting Anita and Billie to rush after her. I murmured quickly to Billie, 'I'll give you your kitten book back if you want to do a project on cats.'

I wasn't quick enough. Cathy had turned round, wondering why Billie wasn't trotting after her obediently.

She frowned. 'What are you two whispering about?' she said.

'I was just asking Billie whether she'd chosen her project,' I said hurriedly.

'She's doing dancing,' Cathy said firmly. Then she gave me an evil grin and pointed at me. 'And we all know what project subject you'll choose, weirdo. Flipping *fairies*!'

Everyone heard. And everyone sniggered. Even Billie. Even *Micky*.

CHAPTER FIVE

I looked in my water glass when I got home. The pressed flower had gone! I supposed Mum had tipped it out – though we'd been in such a rush in the morning surely she hadn't had time to do any washing-up.

'Mum?' I called and went into the big bedroom. She was in her trackie bottoms, pulling an old T-shirt over her head. She was always very careful not to get her maroon overall creased, even when she was tired out.

Robin looked the exact opposite of tired. He was bouncing on the big bed in his socks. This wasn't really allowed as the bed springs were already a bit dodgy.

'Stop that, Robin,' Mum murmured, too exhausted to tell him off properly.

She'd been five minutes late clocking in for work and Mr Henry, the new manager, had given her a ticking-off. He sounded a nightmare. He'd been head of some big office in London but his company had closed and he'd had to get a new job. He sounded very bossy, always telling everyone what to do and how they might improve their work. I imagined him like our Henry vacuum cleaner, barrel-shaped with a little bowler hat and a big booming voice.

I knew Mum was worried that she'd lose her job and then we wouldn't have any money. She yawned as she tried to catch hold of Robin, but he leaped away from her, thinking it was a game.

'Stop thumping about on the bed, Robin! Can't you see Mum's tired,' I said.

'It's not a bed, it's my trampoline, and I'm a circus boy and I'm flying up up up to the ceiling,' said Robin. 'I'm going to do one of those whirly-round head-over-heels things – watch!'

'Don't!' I said sharply, but I was too late.

Robin tucked himself into a little ball and did his best, but he didn't whirl and didn't go head-over-heels. He hurtled

downwards and landed flat on his face. Thank goodness he didn't hurt himself. He lay there, laughing.

Mum rushed to him anxiously.

'He's fine, Mum. Only messing about. Get *off* the bed, Robin, so that Mum can get *on* it and have a little nap,' I said.

'But I'm playing!' said Robin.

'Play with some of your toys,' I said.

Robin sighed heavily but pottered over to the big cardboard box where he kept his toys. He started hauling them all out and found his old pull-along dog right at the bottom.

'I suppose I could be an animal-trainer circus boy,' he declared. 'Here now, Fido, how about learning to walk on your back wheels?'

'Put the other toys back then, Mr Messy. And Mum, you have a little sleep – you look done in,' I said.

Mum protested, but gave in. 'I'll just have a ten-minute nap. Promise you'll wake me then, darling?' she mumbled, flopping onto the duvet.

'OK. Mum, did you fish a flower out of my water glass?'

'No, love,' said Mum, her voice already slurring as she fell asleep.

'Nighty night, then. Or actually afternoony afternoon.

Robin, did you take that flower out of my glass?'

'Nope,' he said, trying to balance Fido. The dog fell over with a thud.

'Why don't you go and train him in the kitchen so Mum can have a bit of peace?' I said.

He trotted off, Fido tucked under his arm, and I went back to my bedroom. I had another peer in my water glass. It was still empty. The flower surely couldn't have dissolved. It was a mystery.

I kicked off my trainers. They were too small now and stubbed the ends of my toes, but it would be the summer holidays soon and I could make do with my flip-flops. I let my toes have a happy wriggle and then felt for my slippers. They were the really girly sort, pink brocade with a very soft fluffy lining, not my type at all, but I had to admit they were very comfy. Well, one was very comfy. The other seemed to have gone a bit lumpy inside and I couldn't get my foot in properly.

'Don't say my slippers are getting too small too!' I muttered to myself.

Something was poking me now, like a sharp little needle. I took the slipper off and peered into it. I nearly dropped it in shock. There was a small person inside, looking indignant.

 69

I blinked. Of course there wasn't a *person* inside my slipper! Some kind of insect? But it seemed to have a fierce little face and long green hair in loose ringlets. Its skin was greenish white, very pale, with a sheen like a pearl. It was shaking violently as if it was desperately cold, though it was adequately clothed, with a little green cap on top of its head and a white gown in a bell shape. Its arms and legs were very spindly, pale green again. It tried to scrabble out of my slipper, but its movements were very feeble. I grabbed it carefully between my thumb and forefinger. I saw it wore little boots with sharp pointy toes.

'Was it *you* poking me?' I whispered.

'You were squashing me, child!' it said indignantly. It looked quite young, about my own age, but it spoke in a tired, peevish way, as if it was an ancient old lady tutting at the manners of children today.

'Wow!' I said. '*Double* wow! You can actually *talk*!'

'Obviously!' it said, tossing its green curls. 'Dear goodness, I've been starved of talk these many years and now I find myself having the most basic conversation with a human noodle. *Wow wow wow!* A dog could introduce more variety into its communication.'

'There's no need to be so rude to me!' I said.

'Well, really – you should make allowances! I'm still very poorly. The last thing a desperate invalid needs is to be attacked in their own bed!' it said.

'It's not your bed. It's my slipper!' I pointed out.

'A slipper? My goodness, I know you are a giant, but you have feet the size of *beds*?' it said incredulously.

'I'm not a giant! I'm one of the smallest in my class. I only seem a giant to you because you're a little insecty person,' I said.

'How dare you call me an insect!' it said, outraged. 'I am a fairy!'

'No you're not! You're not the slightest bit like a fairy. They are sweet – and you're the sourest little thing I've ever come across. You're not even real, anyway. I've obviously fallen asleep like Mum and I'm dreaming you. It's because I looked at my fairy book in the night and saw all those weird pictures. All I have to do is open my eyes and you won't be here,' I declared.

It was bad enough being bullied by Cathy at school. I wasn't going to let myself be tormented by a six-centimetre illusion. I had to wake myself up. I tried opening my eyes really wide, actually pulling the lids apart with my fingers. The creature didn't even blur.

'Why are you pulling faces at me? I'm not the least bit scared,' said the creature, though its tiny hands were clenched. Its pointy feet moved in the air as if it was desperate to run away.

'I'm not going to hurt you. Anyway, you're not real, even though I can't stop dreaming you. I know you can't possibly be a fairy. You're just that old pressed flower that was floating in my water glass,' I said.

'*You* put me in the water?' it said, staring up at me. Its eyes were very big and green. 'Were you trying to drown me?'

'No, of course not! I wouldn't do that! I was trying to plump you up a bit because you were crushed flat. But then I forgot you were in my glass and very nearly swallowed you. I'm sorry about that, but I spat you out almost immediately,' I explained.

The creature stopped its feeble attempts to escape. It went limp, flopping into the palm of my hand.

'Oh, goodness, are you all right? I know it's a pretty

disgusting thought, that you were right in my mouth, but I didn't *bite* you, did I?' I said. 'You can bite me back if I did. If you've got any teeth.'

'Of course I still have teeth, even though I am ancient,' it said weakly, and bared them at me. It didn't still look cross with me though. It was looking up at me almost in awe. 'I've been forced to hibernate like a common bat since some fool crushed me in his book. But now you've brought me back to life!'

'Well, sort of,' I said.

'You rehydrated me and then you put me in your mouth and breathed life into me,' it said.

'I suppose I did,' I agreed. 'Though I wasn't really meaning to.' That sounded a bit ungracious. 'But I'm glad I did.'

'I am truly glad too,' it said. It reached up with one of its fragile little arms and unclenched its fist. 'I am delighted to make your acquaintance.'

I realized it wanted me to shake hands. My own right hand was supporting it, so I tried to shake with the index finger on my left hand, very cautiously so I wouldn't crush it.

'I am pleased to meet you too,' I said, feeling ridiculous. I kept telling myself that obviously I was dreaming, but it was starting to feel very real. I could hear Mum gently snoring in

her bedroom, and Robin's high-pitched voice going, 'Giddy-up, Fido! Good boy!' in the kitchen. I could breathe in the slightly damp smell of our flat, and the sickly lilac of the air-freshener spray. I could feel the twinge in my legs as I kneeled there on the rug, and the flutter and twitch of the tiny creature in my hand.

'So you really *are* a fairy?' I said. 'A girl fairy? You don't look like one. Where are your wings?'

'Let me go and I will show you,' she said.

I opened my hand so that she could stand up. She tidied her long green hair, set her cap straight and smoothed her white dress. Then she took a deep breath. The two folds at the back of her bodice started spreading. They weren't part of her dress at all. They were wings! White wings, with delicate green veins. She spread them to their full extent and stood on her toes. She leaped into the air, dangled a second, started drifting, but with a supreme effort she rose and circled my head. Then she plummeted downwards and landed back in my hand. She lay there, out of breath.

'That was wonderful!' I said.

'It was pathetic,' she gasped. 'I am so out of practice. Oh, my poor wings! They ache so!'

'Have a little rest. What's your name, little fairy?'

'I am actually tall for a fairy,' she said reprovingly. 'You should see the poor bird's-foot trefoil family. They only come up to my kneecaps. *I* am a convolvulus,' she announced.

I blinked at her uncertainly. 'Con . . . what did you say?'

'Convolvulus,' she repeated impatiently. 'Well, I am of the convolvulus family, but there were so few of us left that I'm sure you'll never meet another one.' She sniffed as she spoke, and a tiny tear glistened on her pale cheek.

'I'm very sorry, Con . . . Convon . . . Convonuseless?'

She sighed deeply, though she was so small she hardly made a sound. 'Perhaps you'd better call me by my common name. I am Bindweed.'

'Bindweed? I thought fairies had names like . . . like Sparkle or Twinkletoes,' I said.

Bindweed shuddered. 'Please!' she said. 'I come from a very long line of aristocratic flower fairy folk. We were singing in our picturesque bowers when you human folk were still grunting in caves.' Mum was still snoring next door. 'Some of you have yet to get past that stage,' Bindweed added unkindly.

'Don't be so mean!' I said indignantly. 'Poor Mum's exhausted. She sometimes needs to have a little nap. But I'm

going to wake her up now and she will be so so so thrilled to meet you, Bindweed. She absolutely loves fairies! You should see all the fairy stuff in the living room! She even goes to special fairy fairs and emails all these other fairy-lovers. They'll be so dead jealous if they hear she's met a real fairy!'

'No! Don't wake her! And you mustn't tell her about me! You absolutely mustn't! My life depends on it!' Bindweed was shaking again, tugging her own hair in her anxiety.

'But my mum's lovely. She wouldn't dream of hurting you! She'd be in total awe of you,' I said.

'She'd tell her friends. Then they'd blab to the newspapers and I'd be kept in captivity as a freakish curiosity,' she said, sounding terrified. 'These tales of horror are legend in the fairy world. Even girls like you betray us.'

'I would never do that! And Mum wouldn't either. She'd keep you a secret if you asked her. I promise,' I said. But I couldn't be sure I *could* trust Mum. I knew how excited she'd get. She'd want to share her amazing discovery. And I worried that she'd get upset. Bindweed could be very direct at times.

I heard Robin crashing about in the kitchen, apparently trying to make Fido jump through an imaginary hoop.

'Jump, Fido, jump!' he said.

There was an almighty thump as Fido failed, and then high-pitched furious barking. Bindweed nearly fell off my hand.

'A dog! You have a dog! Hide me!' she cried, clinging to my fingers.

'It's not a real dog! It's only my little brother being silly playing with his old toy dog,' I said.

Mum's snoring had stopped. 'Robin? Did you fall over? Are you playing with Mab?' she called.

I clasped Bindweed as gently as I could, bent down and popped her back into my slipper. I put it in the dark underneath my bed and then straightened up as Mum burst into my room.

'It's OK, Mum. Robin's playing in the kitchen. You go back to sleep,' I said reassuringly.

'No, no, I was only going to nap for a minute or two,' said Mum, standing up and rubbing the back of her neck. She yawned. 'What sort of dozy mum am I, eh? I'll get supper started, pet – you must be starving.'

She hurried off to check on Robin.

'I'd better go and help her,' I whispered under the bed. 'I won't say a word about you. You go back to sleep for a bit.'

'Did I hear the huge mother say "supper"?' Bindweed hissed.

'She's not huge! She's small and slim,' I said. 'Will you stop being so rude about my mum!'

'But she *is* huge! And so are you. I know you can't help it, but, like any humans I have ever seen, you're both such enormous, lumbering creatures it's a wonder you don't topple over,' she insisted.

'And you're a weeny, squitty little thing with no manners whatsoever!' I retorted.

There was no reply until I'd reached the door, one slipper on and one slipper off. I walked a little lopsidedly now, but I certainly didn't *lumber*.

'Supper?' said a faint but insistent voice from under the bed.

I felt like ignoring her, but I supposed she must be feeling ravenous after spending years trapped in an old book. 'I'll see what I can do,' I said, and then went to join Mum and Robin.

Mum was putting fish fingers under the grill and opening a tin of baked beans. I liked fish fingers and baked beans, but I wasn't sure it was really fairy fare.

'Where's your other slipper?' Mum asked.

'Oh, my toes were feeling a bit squashed so I'm letting them have a good wriggle,' I said.

'Oh dear. I suppose we'll have to get you new slippers now, as well as new trainers,' Mum said anxiously. She muttered to herself as she tipped the beans into a saucepan, and I knew she was working out how much both would cost and subtracting the amount from her monthly wage. It wouldn't leave much for ordinary everyday things, especially as Mum had just bought my awful fairy dress. I was sure Bindweed would be withering if I dressed up in it.

I gazed at the picture Mum had hung on the kitchen wall. She'd found it at a car boot sale, a picture of fairies skipping around a ring of toadstools. They were all sweetly pretty creatures, with golden hair or gloriously dark curls, and sparkly frocks and gossamer wings. There wasn't a single one who had limp green ringlets and a droopy dress and a very fierce face.

Mum saw me peering at it. She smiled. 'It's such a pretty picture, isn't it?' she said.

'Mm,' I said, though I much preferred the weird paintings in my birthday-present book. 'Mum, what do you think fairies eat?'

Mum thought about it. 'Nectar?' she suggested.

'What exactly *is* nectar?' I asked.

'It's the stuff you get inside flowers,' Mum said vaguely. 'I think it's a bit like honey.'

'Oh!' I said, remembering the jar of honey.

'And they eat those little cakes with icing and rainbow sprinkles,' said Robin.

'Oh, *fairy* cakes! Clever boy!' said Mum. She paused, thinking it through. 'Would you like us to try making some?'

'Oh, yes please!' said Robin.

'That would be great,' I said, though I didn't think they were called fairy cakes because actual fairies liked to eat them. And one fairy cake would be enough to feed a whole flock of fairies. It would be rock hard by the time Bindweed had finished it. It would be like me trying to eat my way through a giant sponge cake big enough for me to sit on.

'I'll give it a go tomorrow,' said Mum. 'Or the next day. When we've finished up the birthday cake.'

We ate a slice each for pudding, after the fish fingers and baked beans. I insisted on clearing the table. I managed to pop a tiny portion of fish, a pink icing rosette and a very small crust of bread dipped into the honey jar inside the pocket of my school skirt. While Mum was making up a story about Fido for

Robin, I sauntered casually to the bedroom, muttering something about my slipper.

I kneeled down and peered into the darkness under the bed. 'Supper time!' I whispered.

Bindweed came scuttling out, covered with that weird grey fluffy stuff that gathers under the bed no matter how often you sweep it. She plucked it off her white dress disdainfully.

'I need a proper dewdrop bath!' she demanded.

'Well, have some supper first,' I said. 'And I wish you wouldn't treat me like a servant all the time. Aren't I the person who brought you back to life?'

'I beg your pardon,' said Bindweed, more humbly. 'So, what have you made me for my supper?'

I felt in my pocket, which was unpleasantly sticky now. I held out my hand. Bindweed's supper had got rather mashed together. She peered at the flakes of fish, the crumbled pink icing and the honey crust.

'That's supper?' she said weakly.

'I'm sorry. It was the best I could do at short notice,' I said.

I found a couple of Lego bricks and spread the fish on one and the pink icing on the other as daintily as I could. The crust of honey wouldn't balance so I propped it against another

brick. Bindweed looked at them in horror but managed not to say anything. She sat cross-legged and picked up a tiny flake of fish.

'What is it?' she asked.

'It's a fish finger,' I said.

'A fish *finger*?' she repeated, waggling her own fingers.

'It's not a real finger. Of course fish don't have actual fingers. It's just what it's called,' I explained.

Bindweed ate the weeniest morsel. She chewed at it valiantly and tried to swallow. She started choking. I was horrified and rushed for my water glass. She had to grip it with both small hands and dunk her head in. Her hair got very wet, but she managed to drink enough to wash the tiny fish flake down.

'Thank you,' she murmured weakly, detaching herself from the glass.

'I take it you don't like fish fingers?' I said.

'I'm afraid not,' said Bindweed. 'In fact, it was positively disgusting.'

'I'm sorry,' I said meekly. 'Try the icing rosette. You might like it more.'

She looked very wary but she seemed to like the smell of it.

She tried to take a bite but found it impossible, though her tiny teeth looked very sharp. She licked it instead but didn't make much progress. However, the honey crust was a success. She couldn't manage the crust itself, but she held it like a gigantic baguette and sucked at it eagerly.

'Careful! I don't want you choking again!' I said. 'But I'm so glad you like it.'

'It's honey!' said Bindweed. She smacked her small lips together. 'Clover honey – my favourite.'

She sucked the crust dry and sat back happily. Her cheeks had flushed the palest pink. 'Thank you very much, girl,' she said.

'My name's Mab,' I said.

'Mab!' Bindweed gasped.

'Yes, I know it's a weird name. I've never met anyone else called Mab,' I said.

'*I* have!' said Bindweed. 'It was the name of our wondrous queen. Of *all* our queens, generation after generation, since time immemorial. We were all aware that the last Queen Mab sadly perished long ago, but when I was just a tiny bud of a fairy my mother held me in her arms and we watched the queen's carriage pass through the Royal Rose Bower. I saw her golden crown and her beautiful rose-coloured gown.' She looked at me hopefully. 'You don't have a golden crown, do you?'

'No, I don't,' I said regretfully. But my mind was whirling. It would be such *fun* to pretend to be a fairy queen . . .

'I thought not,' said Bindweed.

'But I do have a pink fairy dress,' I said, suddenly excited.

'No you don't,' said Bindweed.

'I do, I do!' I said triumphantly. 'Right, close your eyes and I'll put it on.'

'This isn't a trick, is it?' Bindweed asked. 'Are you going to grab me and crush me within the pages of a book?'

'Would I do that when I've gone to all this trouble to revive you?' I said. I'd done it accidentally, but it was true enough all the same.

'I suppose not,' said Bindweed. 'Very well, I'll close my eyes.'

She shut them tight. I whipped off my school dress, went to my wardrobe and pulled on my fairy dress, stretching out the wings and fluffing out the skirts.

'There! You can open your eyes now,' I said.

Bindweed opened them wide. I thought she'd giggle at me. I'd only put the dress on to prove my point. But she looked utterly taken aback. She scrambled to her feet, held out the hem of her white frock and curtsied to me!

CHAPTER SIX

I thought Bindweed was mocking me. I could see the reflection of myself in the looking glass. My white face with the pink nose, just like a little white rat. My long pale straggly hair. My spindly arms and legs. My big feet. My bright pink dress with limp wings. Some fairy!

Yet Bindweed was very pale too, and her nose was pink with excitement. Her green ringlets straggled. Her arms and legs were so spindly they looked in danger of snapping, and her feet in her green pointy shoes were the largest part of her. Her dress was white but she had said Queen Mab wore a rose-coloured dress. My wings didn't work –

but Bindweed didn't know that, did she?

Did she truly think I was a fairy queen? Surely I was fifty times too tall! Bindweed craned her neck, looking me up and down. This was clearly troubling her too.

'Why are you so elongated, Your Majesty?' she asked.

I thought hard. 'A witch put a wicked spell on me,' I said, thinking up a story fast. I really wanted her to believe I was a fairy queen. She'd maybe show me some respect then!

Bindweed frowned. 'Please don't tease me,' she said.

'As if I'd do that,' I said. 'It's true. It's most unfortunate, but there's no way the spell can be broken. The witch sent my father, the king, into exile and then put a spell on my mother and my brother too. So we have to live as human beings and lumber about like them.' I was getting quite carried away. I could even see this witch, her face distorted with malice, her crooked finger pointing at us as she cast her spell.

But Bindweed put her hands on her hips and shook her small head at me. 'There are no such things as witches,' she said sternly. 'They are human women who practise herbal medicine and act as midwives. They might have broomsticks in their humble cottages but they are for sweeping the hearth. They cannot fly. They keep evil black cats, to be avoided at all costs, but they cannot cast spells. I am not a little child to be fobbed off with nonsense, Queen Mab.'

I swallowed hard. 'You must have faith, little Bindweed,' I said grandly. 'We fairies must flock together.'

Bindweed seemed to be losing faith rapidly. 'Tell me about your Royal Protocol,' she said suspiciously.

I didn't know what the word *protocol* meant. Did she mean duties and routine? What *would* fairy queens do all day, when they weren't being driven around in golden carriages? Bindweed wasn't going to be impressed with an account of my own day-to-day life, either at home or at school. I tried to translate it:

'I take counsel with the dear Queen Mother and I assist the little Crown Prince,' I said. 'I study hard and battle with unruly commoners. I am amused by Micky, the court jester,' I said. 'Plus I rescue small fairies who have been imprisoned in books,' I added for good measure.

'Mm,' said Bindweed. She circled me, peering up at my wings. 'And do you fly often?'

'When the mood takes me,' I replied cautiously.

'Then fly now,' she said.

'But I'm *not* in the mood now,' I said. 'I'm very tired.'

88

'Just fly up to the ceiling and back, like this,' said Bindweed. She spread her own wings and flapped them a little. Drops of water made a minute puddle on the rug. She still hadn't dried out properly from her dunk in the water glass. She had to flap hard for a moment or two, her face screwed up with effort, but at last she gathered strength, and her wings shone. She stood on tiptoe in her pointy green boots and took off, whirling upwards in the air with a strange small hum like a tiny mosquito. She buzzed around my head, even landing on my shoulder for a second, smiling at me, her green eyes gleaming. Then she flew down and down in a spiral and landed gracefully, her white dress belling out around her.

'There!' she gasped, breathing heavily. 'Now it's your turn.'

'I'm out of practice,' I said quickly.

'I'm pretty sure you haven't been crushed in a book for years like me – but I managed it,' said Bindweed.

'There's not enough room. I'll hit my head on the ceiling,' I protested.

Bindweed looked at me with contempt. 'Excuses, excuses,' she said. 'You can't fly, can you? You're not any kind of fairy, let alone a new Queen Mab. You're simply a pathetic impostor.'

She was beginning to sound like a tiny version of Cathy. I
started to tremble. 'I'll show you!' I said, and I took a gigantic
leap upwards, arms outspread. I hoped that somehow sheer
determination would power me up into the air, even if I
couldn't quite reach the ceiling. I failed miserably. My wings
didn't even flap. I went crashing downwards and landed in a
heap on the carpet.

'Mab? Are you all right, darling?' Mum called from the
living room. She came rushing in to check – while Bindweed
scuttled under the bed. 'How did you fall over?' Mum asked
anxiously. 'Have you hurt yourself?'

'I'm fine, Mum,' I said, getting to my feet.

'You're wearing your fairy dress!' said Mum, sounding
tremendously pleased. 'I wasn't sure you really liked it.'

'Well, I do. Really,' I said. 'It makes me feel like a fairy
queen.'

'Oh, darling!' Mum gave me a hug. 'So where does it hurt?'

'Nowhere! I was just dancing about and tripped over my
own big feet,' I said.

'Probably because you've got one slipper on and one slipper
off!' said Mum. 'Better put the other one on now, pet.'

'I – I'm not sure where it is,' I said.

'You've probably kicked it under the bed,' said Mum.

'Let me look!' I said urgently, and practically pushed her out of the way. I peered under the bed. Bindweed had climbed into my slipper again and was huddled inside.

I picked her up as gently as I could with my thumb and forefinger. She waggled her skinny arms and legs in protest as I deposited her on the floor and pulled my slipper out into the daylight.

'Here it is!' I said.

'Pop it on then and come and watch a bit of telly with Robin and me,' said Mum. 'It's nearly time.'

Mum didn't watch the news at six o'clock. She hated seeing anything worrying or upsetting. She watched quiz shows instead – sometimes I thought she liked them even more than her fairies! She liked *House of Games* most of all. She didn't guess many of the answers. She just liked watching Richard Osman because he was so kind and gentle. She chatted to him while he was on.

'That's right, you keep them guessing, Richard! You're so clever and you know so much. But you look a bit tired today. No wonder – you work so hard! Yet you keep smiling, don't you, pet?' she murmured. It was as if he was part of our family.

Robin used to think he could really hear us and would say hello and goodbye to him and wave.

I sat on the sofa with Mum and Robin and Fido, and imagined having a chat with Richard Osman myself: *Hi, Richard, do you happen to know anything about fairies? I mean, I know they don't exist, but the thing is, there's a real one underneath my bed. She's not actually very nice – she's very grumpy and bosses me around, but I think that's because she's worried. I'm so big and she's so tiny and scared of being squashed. She's made me swear not to tell anyone about her, but it doesn't count talking to you inside my head because you can't actually hear me. So what am I going to do about her?*

Richard smiled on the television and said cheerfully, 'Well, shall we find out the right answer?'

I wished he could. I pretended I needed to go to the loo, and dashed into the bedroom instead. I kneeled down and peered under the bed. I couldn't see anything at all for a moment and panicked – but then I saw Bindweed had wrapped herself in one of the little rolls of dust, wearing it like a shawl. I could just see her green cap and her pointy green boots sticking out at either end.

'Bindweed?' I whispered. 'It's all right – it's only me, Mab.'

She didn't answer. She was making a tiny sound, like the weeniest sniffles.

'Oh, don't cry!' I whispered. I put my hand out to try to reassure her, but she scurried further under the bed.

'I haven't told Mum and Robin about you, I promise. I'm going to look after you and keep you safe,' I murmured.

There was another tiny sniff. 'I don't *want* you to look after me!' she sobbed. 'I am at least a hundred and seventy years older than you – probably more.'

I wasn't sure this could possibly be true. Nobody lived to that extreme age. It would make her a . . . *Victorian!* We'd been learning about them at school. But Bindweed wasn't just anybody: she was a fairy.

'Still, I'm much bigger and stronger than you are,' I said. 'And I can bring you honey and water, and you can sleep in my slipper and hide under the bed.'

'That's not much of a life!' Bindweed wept. 'I'll be your prisoner! I've already been trapped in that book for so many years and now you want to lock me up again!'

I had to agree she had a point.

'You'll have the flat to yourself during the day, though. There are all sorts of things you'll like, special fairy things, you wait and see. You'll be able to sit on a chair exactly the right size and jump up and down on a toadstool and dip your toe in a fairy pool. I could even fill it with dew. There! You couldn't have found a better home. We've got a hundred and one fairy things. It's practically Fairyland already. And I'm Queen Mab, right?'

'Wrong!' Bindweed hissed. 'You can't fly!'

'Well, perhaps I can't right at the moment. I'm in human disguise, see. Humans can't fly, so my wings have lost their power and gone all droopy, so of course I can't fly just like that. *You* found it pretty difficult at first, didn't you? And there's so much more of me now, so it's harder for me to stop being earthbound. But inside I'm little and light and still a fairy – a fairy *queen*.'

'Nonsense,' said Bindweed, venturing out from under the bed.

'I'll prove it,' I said, thinking fast. I didn't think most people in Victorian days had electricity. And if she had been trapped later, well, she had been living outdoors . . . I ran to the light switch. 'I can make the sun come out with one flick of my finger!' I said and demonstrated.

Light flooded the room. Bindweed reeled backwards, screwing her eyes up.

'Have you set the room on fire, you mad giant?' she cried. 'Douse me in your water glass!'

'There's no need to panic. It's not fire, I promise. It's only light. Magic light. And I can make it disappear with a flick of my finger,' I said, and I touched the switch again. 'See, now it's gone. And yet I can make it come back. It's magic, isn't it? Admit it, Bindweed!' I said triumphantly.

She sniffed. 'It's some devious trickery,' she said. 'Repeat it if you can!'

'Certainly,' I said. 'OK, on! And now off! On! Off! On! Off!'

'Mab! Are you mucking about with the light?' Mum called from the living room. 'Don't do that, darling, you'll

fuse it! We don't need the light on at all yet – it's not dark.'

'Sorry, Mum,' I called.

'Are you coming back to watch telly with us?' she asked.

'In a minute,' I yelled. Aha! Television! I was pretty certain they didn't have televisions in Fairyland. I bent down to Bindweed's level. 'Let me carry you into the room next door. You will see little people that I've enchanted. I've made them tiny, not much bigger than you, and squashed them inside a big flat box. Mum and Robin love to watch them.'

'You're talking nonsense,' Bindweed said. 'This is a trap. You just want to show me to them and then *I'll* be squashed into a box for people to gawp at.'

'I told you, I'm not going to show you to anyone. I promise, promise, promise. Look, let me pick you up and put you down my top. You can hide there when we go into the living room and peep out when it's safe.'

I'm quite skinny and the fairy costume was on the big side. There was plenty of room. I held out the top of the bodice invitingly. 'Come on, Bindweed, hop in!'

She shook her head fiercely, backing away from me, but I made a sudden grab at her and stuffed her down my dress before she could escape. She struggled violently, trying to

climb out, but I clamped my hand over the little lump near my waistband – not hard enough to hurt her, simply to keep her still.

'Let me out!' she shrieked, trying to kick me with her pointy boots.

'Ssh, now. You don't want Mum and Robin to hear you, do you?' I said, and ran into the living room.

I felt Bindweed flatten herself right at the bottom of the bodice, just above the waistband. She was trying to stay still but I could feel her trembling. I felt horribly mean, but I knew I wasn't really putting her at any risk. Mum and Robin were glued to the television, cuddled up on the sofa. Robin had Fido on his lap so that he could hardly see the screen let alone me. Fido's wheels were pressing down on his bare legs, which must have been uncomfortable, but Robin didn't seem to mind. He didn't know the answer to any of Richard's games but cheerily shouted out nonsense each time.

Mum didn't know many answers either but didn't let it get her down. Whenever Richard Osman looked directly at the camera and asked how we at home were getting on, Mum would giggle. 'Oh, Richard, you know what I'm like with geography,' she'd say. 'And it's no use asking me about pop

songs – I'm rubbish at that.'

She smiled when she saw me. 'Here's our little fairy!' she said.

I heard the smallest shriek inside my bodice. Bindweed clearly thought she'd been spotted.

'Yes, I'm your fairy – Mab,' I said quickly, twirling around so they wouldn't spot Bindweed scurrying about frantically.

Mum patted the space on the sofa. 'Come and cuddle up with us, Mab,' she said.

'I don't want to crush my lovely fairy frock,' I said, sitting on the armchair beside them and spreading my skirts primly.

They could only see me sideways there, and if Bindweed suddenly tried to make a bolt for freedom I'd have more chance of stopping her without them seeing.

I clasped my hands lightly over the tiny lump of Bindweed, stroking her with the tips of my fingers. I felt little pokes, as if she was trying to brush them aside. But after a few minutes she quietened, though she still felt very tense. I knew she was listening. She could hear Mum. She could hear Robin. She could hear Robin make Fido bark. But she could also hear Richard Osman and his four contestants.

Bindweed started stealthily climbing upwards inside my bodice. She paused right at the top for a full two minutes, and then I felt her ringlets tickling me as she poked her head right out above the satin. She jerked violently when she saw the television. Little people inside my magic box!

She pressed back against my chest. Perhaps she really thought I'd trap her inside the television too. She watched intently, starting whenever any music was played, and ducked down at the end of the show when they played the signature tune.

'Can I pick a programme now, Mum?' I asked.

She threw me the remote. I flicked through channel after channel, showing off my 'magic powers' to Bindweed. I craftily

chose an animal programme set in Africa. Bindweed trembled as lions roared and elephants trumpeted. I didn't want to scare her too much, so I channel-hopped again to a cartoon on children's television. This seemed to startle her even more. But it was an advert that got the most reaction from her. An advert for washing-up liquid.

She was so furious she threw away all sense of caution. 'That *abomination* is not a fairy!' she declared.

She had only a tiny voice but Mum heard.

'What did you say, Mab? I didn't quite catch it,' she said, turning her head to me.

Bindweed scooted down my bodice again.

'Oh, I was just – just pretending to be a fairy,' I said.

'You are sweet, darling! It's lovely that you're really getting into the whole fairy world now. But fairies would never ever talk like that, in little screechy voices! I've never been lucky enough to hear one, of course, but they say they talk in this wonderful melodic way, rather like the tinkling of bells,' said Mum.

'Oh! Is that right?' I said, hardly able to keep a straight face. If only Mum knew she'd heard a real fairy just then! I ached to tell her – it would mean the whole world to her. But I couldn't betray Bindweed. I wasn't sure I even *liked*

Bindweed, because she was so rude and demanding, and I was certain she couldn't stand me, but I felt compelled to protect her all the same.

She was keeping totally still and silent now, curled into a tight little ball. I cupped my hands very carefully over her – and this time she didn't poke me. She stayed still, and very slowly I felt her spread out a little, relaxing.

At seven o'clock Mum went off to bath Robin. He was probably old enough to bath himself, but he still needed supervision to make sure he didn't simply play fountains with an old shampoo bottle rather than scrubbing himself. When I heard the bath taps running and Robin's giggles as Mum tickled him, I gave Bindweed a little pat.

'It's OK. They'll be gone ages. Shall I show you around the living room? It's got a lot of fairy stuff – but I'm not sure you'll approve,' I whispered down my fairy-dress front.

Bindweed climbed upwards and emerged, her hair sticking up wildly, her white dress crushed, her wings as limp as my own.

'Oh dear,' I said, standing her on the palm of my hand. I did my best to tidy her up with my other hand, arranging her curls and smoothing out the creases from her dress. She

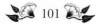

flapped her wings herself until they spread out, the delicate green veins glowing.

'Thank you,' she said, surprisingly meekly.

She peered around the room, astonished.

'I can make it prettier,' I said, and I carried her over to the fairy lights switch. I put them on to flash mode, turning it up high.

Mum loved it when they flashed very rapidly because your eyes started to play tricks and you could really believe you saw a fairy in the dazzle. Robin and I liked it too because it was like a disco party and we could dance around wildly in the sparkling light. I hoped Bindweed might like it as well.

She gave a small cry of pain and bent double, putting her hands over her eyes. 'You're blinding me!' she gasped. 'Ooh, I feel so sick!' She clutched her tiny tummy and groaned.

'I'm so so sorry,' I said, switching them off. 'Just lie still a moment with your eyes closed. I didn't realize the effect they would have on you – but of course it must feel totally over-powering when you have such small eyes.'

'Indeed,' Bindweed murmured. Then she rallied a little. 'Actually many fairy folk tell me my eyes are my finest feature because they are so *big*,' she added.

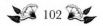

'Yes, but they're like little beady insect eyes compared to mine,' I said.

'Are you comparing me to an insect *again*?' Bindweed demanded. 'How dare you! Such lowly revolting creatures!' Well, Mum had a flock of pewter fairies riding ladybirds and grasshoppers along the windowsill, but fairies and insects clearly didn't get along in real fairy life.

I still couldn't quite believe in Bindweed, even though there she was in front of my eyes, flopping about in my hand and yawning with nausea. I could see her, I could feel her, I could hear her, I could even smell her. I'd thought fairies would smell of roses, like the fairy potion Mum had sent for once on the internet. We'd thought it didn't smell too bad at first, but the pale golden colour darkened very quickly. It soon reeked of stagnant water and Mum had to throw it away. After that, she made her own, out of rosewater and glycerine.

Bindweed didn't smell rosy – or stagnant, thank goodness. She had a strange, fresh, earthy sort of smell, like rain and wind and grass. It was very slight but distinct, and I rather liked it. I bent nearer to take a deep breath of it.

'Don't!' Bindweed screamed.

'Don't what?' I asked.

'Come so close to me! It's horrible!' she said.

'I only wanted to look at you properly, that's all,' I said, really hurt. Did she think *I* was horrible?

'You looked as if you might swallow me,' said Bindweed.

'As if I'd do that,' I said.

'Well, you said you nearly did exactly that!' Bindweed snapped.

'That was a total accident. And I didn't swallow you – I spat you straight out,' I said. 'And it was like I was giving you the kiss of life. I thought you were grateful.'

'I am,' Bindweed conceded reluctantly.

'You should be extra polite to me anyway because I am your fairy queen,' I said.

'So you say,' said Bindweed.

'I can do magic tricks, can't I?' I said.

'So can the Lord of Darkness,' said Bindweed, 'and he is an expert shapeshifter.'

I blinked at her. She didn't seriously think I was the *devil*, did she? The thought made me feel really powerful.

'I think you should be extra respectful then, just in case,' I said. 'So, I'll give you a grand tour of the living room now.'

Poor Mum. Bindweed was unimpressed with all her

precious fairy ornaments. In fact, she shuddered several times. She thought the little pewter fairies hideous and pulled faces at them. I invited her to sit down on one of the little twig chairs Mum had made so painstakingly, but she said it was much too hard and she might get splinters. She didn't even like the beautiful little fairy house with a roof carved to look like ivy leaves.

'I can't abide *Hedera*,' she said. 'Its common name is ivy. And it *is* common. Nasty, creeping, sinister stuff.' She peered inside the latticed window. 'It isn't furnished inside!' she complained. She tried pushing the little wooden door. 'You can't even open it!' she added. 'What's the point of a home you can't get into?'

'Perhaps I could make you a proper home,' I said.

I was quite good at making things out of cardboard boxes. Mum often carted several home from the supermarket because they were simply put out for recycling. She used them for extra storage as our furniture was a bit sparse. I could squash all my T-shirts and socks and knickers into just one box and use the other to make a fairy house for Bindweed. I could let her keep my slipper for her bed and use tissues as a ready supply of clean sheets. Maybe I could build her a table out of Lego? But how could I make her a soft chair? And a bath? And what did fairies do when they needed to go to the toilet? Bindweed was such a picky little creature. If she turned her nose up at Mum's lovingly made fairy furniture, she'd find mine very makeshift.

'It's kind of you to suggest making me a home,' said Bindweed. 'But I *have* a home. Now that I'm rested and recovered, please will you take me there?'

CHAPTER SEVEN

'Where's your home, Bindweed?' I asked.

'I live on the Wentworth estate,' she said proudly.

'On the *Wentworth estate*?' I repeated, astonished.

There were lots of blocks of flats in our town – and some of them were lovely – but the Wentworth estate was like a grim concrete fortress, with burnt-out cars and piles of rubbish in the grounds. There were nice kids there, of course, but some of the Wentworth kids would beat you up if you dared even look at them. Their dogs were all illegal fighting breeds and might tear you to shreds if you went anywhere near them. The Wentworth gangs didn't just have knives – they had guns.

I hadn't actually seen any of this for myself. I would never have dared put one foot into Wentworth territory. But I was certain it was all true.

'Are you sure you mean the actual Wentworth estate – the one up Fairmount Hill?' I asked.

'Yes, of course,' said Bindweed. She clutched hold of my finger earnestly. 'You will take me there, won't you? I'm not sure I could manage to fly all the way by myself and I might get confused. I haven't lived there for so long. Indeed, I haven't lived at all for many years. I've been squashed between the pages of a book in a state of suspension! Please please please take me back to dear Wentworth!'

'I'm not sure the Wentworth estate is quite how you're remembering it. It's a bit . . . wild now,' I said.

'I am a member of the convolvulus family! We embrace wildness. Given our way, we'd turn every ornamental garden into a delightful tangle. Oh, I'm faint with longing! Please can we go there immediately?'

'We can't go there now – it's nearly bedtime,' I said. I imagined going to the Wentworth estate at night, when the gangs were prowling!

'Oh, for goodness' sake! You're as bad as my pretentious

cousin, Morning Glory. Ridiculous name!' Bindweed said, a little enviously. 'She wilts in the afternoon and curls up fast asleep until sunrise, the idle wench. Very well. First thing tomorrow.'

'I have to go to school!'

'A great girl like you still goes to school? You're not exactly a tiny bud, are you?' said Bindweed.

'I wish you'd stop being so mean to me. It's especially silly when you're trying to get me to do something for you,' I said. I heard a swoosh from the bathroom and Robin's chuckles as Mum lifted him out and wrapped him up in a towel. 'Look, we'll have to discuss it later. It's my turn to have a bath now.'

'I like to have my bath in the morning dew,' said Bindweed. 'I can't wait to be out of doors. It's so stuffy in this home of yours. I don't know how you bear it. I feel faint for lack of air!' She gave a great yawn, which ended in a frightened gulp because Mum put her head round the door.

'Have you got hiccups?' said Mum, as Bindweed dived down my bodice. 'You're clutching your chest! Does it hurt?'

'No, no, I'm fine,' I said quickly.

'Well, time for your bath now, darling. I'm just putting Robin into his jim-jams,' said Mum.

'Coming.'

Bindweed had to come with me whether she wanted to or not. The bathroom was hot and steamy now, like a tropical jungle. Mum always let me have a long bath in peace. I usually liked to read, with my head propped up comfortably on a rolled-up towel, though sometimes the towel slipped and fell in the water, and once or twice the book dropped in too, which made the pages ripple afterwards.

There was no chance of a peaceful read with Bindweed around. I fished her out of my fairy dress and sat her in the soap dish. It had a fairy pattern, inevitably. Bindweed wrinkled her nose at it but liked the smell of the soap.

'It reminds me of a friend of mine, dear Honeysuckle,' she said, sighing. 'Oh, I can't wait to see all my friends again! I'm even looking forward to seeing Morning Glory. I won't go as far as Ivy, though. He is my worst-ever enemy.'

'I have one of those,' I said. 'Her name's Cathy and she's mean to me. Even meaner than you.'

'I won't be the slightest bit mean if you take me home to Wentworth tomorrow,' said Bindweed. '*Please* say you'll do so?' She clasped her tiny hands imploringly.

'I'll have to think about it,' I said, topping up Robin's bath with hot water and shaking in lots of bubble bath.

Bindweed could feel the steam on her face. 'A *hot* waterfall!' she said, fanning herself extravagantly.

'Yes, and I can make it stop just like this,' I said, turning off the tap.

She looked moderately impressed. But then I had to get *in* the bath. I felt ridiculously shy getting undressed in front of Bindweed. She would stare so. I had no idea what fairy bodies were like under their dresses, but surely they were pretty similar to mine? My fairy dress looked pathetic crumpled on the bathmat. The label showed, saying FAIRY PRINCESS. The wings were obviously made of cheap gauzy material stretched over thin bendy wire. Bindweed's own beautiful wings twitched slightly, as if in contempt.

Running water always makes me desperate to go to the toilet, and that was even more embarrassing with Bindweed's beady eyes fixed on me. I flushed the toilet quickly, hoping she would think it another magic trick, and jumped in the bath. Bindweed was splashed a little bit and clearly wasn't pleased, but kept quiet for a minute or two. Then she started up a very tiny mumbling. I couldn't hear her properly at first – it was just a little insect whine – but it got louder.

'Please take me home to Wentworth tomorrow! Please take me home!

I will die of longing if you don't take me! Please please please! You've saved my life once, O magical Mab. Please save me again and take me home tomorrow!'

It got louder and louder. She seemed to be droning right inside my ear. The noise went round and round inside my head, driving me crazy.

'All right!' I said. 'Just stop that awful noise!'

She stopped immediately.

'You promise?' she demanded.

'If I can,' I said warily.

'You can do anything if you're a fairy queen,' said Bindweed.

'Don't push it,' I said. I scooped some frothy bathwater onto my hands and blew a stream of bubbles at her.

She squealed and tried to catch one. It disappeared and she looked so surprised

I laughed out loud.

'Do it again!' she said.

I blew and blew and she watched  the bubbles, enchanted. She left her little soap dish throne and started flying through the air, popping the bubbles with her tiny fingers, laughing too. It seemed so weird to be playing a game with an ancient and extremely cantankerous fairy.

'Exactly how old are you, Bindweed?' I asked.

She shrugged her small shoulders. 'I am over one hundred and fifty years old. Possibly one hundred and eighty? I could even be two hundred. I know your queen was on the throne when I was born.'

'Queen Elizabeth?' I said.

'I am not *that* old!' said Bindweed. 'But we are all taught about Queen Elizabeth when we are seedlings. She was a great and glorious personage. She was even given the honorary title of Fairy Queen, though of course human blood ran in her veins.'

'I think that was maybe the first Queen Elizabeth,' I said. We had learned about the Tudors at school. I tried to think of another queen. 'Queen Victoria?' I suggested.

'That's the very one,' said Bindweed.

'So you truly are a *real* Victorian! Oh, Bindweed, can you tell me all about the Victorian age? I've got to do a special project for Mrs Horsley at school. She'd be dead impressed if I did the Victorians.'

'Well, humans were much the same then as now. I didn't have much to do with them, like all sensible fairies. Either the huge gruff ones stamp on you with their heavy boots or the small soft ones grab at you and try to keep you in a matchbox. I hid in the hedgerow whenever any came near. Even the fine folk in Wentworth House were uncouth sometimes, making merry till all hours and playing music loud enough to scare the birds,' said Bindweed, shaking her head. 'Especially when I was older, and all the young humans seemed to do little but dance and have parties.'

It certainly sounded much the same. I'd heard about the all-night raves at Wentworth. I wasn't sure where this hedgerow was. But it definitely didn't seem the sort of place to go bird-spotting. The Wentworth gang, I'd been told, would use any

stray starling or sparrow for target practice. Or any child, come to that.

I shivered, even though my bath was still hot.

It was so worrying that I couldn't sleep properly that night. Mum and Robin were tucked up together fast asleep in the big bed. Bindweed wasn't stirring in the slipper under my little bed. I tossed and turned, trying to work out what to do.

I couldn't ask Mum to come for a stroll around the Wentworth estate before or after school. She'd think I'd lost the plot. She wouldn't take Robin or me there in a million years. She didn't even let me play outside in our road because she thought some of the children were too rough. And I couldn't possibly go there by myself either. It was much too scary. I'd simply have to make it plain to Bindweed that it was far too dangerous. She couldn't *make* me take her. I didn't have to do what she said, even if she was a fairy. I wasn't scared of *her*, was I?

Well, I suppose I was, just a little bit.

It seemed ridiculous to be frightened of a tiny creature no bigger than a mouse. She was little and helpless, for all her bossy ways. She couldn't do anything bad to me. It only tickled when she poked me with her little fingers and kicked me with

her pointy boots. But if she was a real fairy – and there was no doubting that now – it meant she was magic. Maybe she could cast a spell on me? A wicked enchantment, like the bad fairy in the Sleeping Beauty story?

I wasn't a beauty and we didn't have any spindles, whatever they were, so I couldn't prick my finger on one – but it would almost be a relief to be put to sleep for a hundred years because I hadn't slept a wink for most of the night and I was desperately tired. I tried to think of other wicked spells. Wasn't there a story about a proud girl who upset a fairy and had toads come spilling out of her mouth whenever she opened it? That sounded pretty disgusting – but I could always aim them at Cathy if she was being particularly mean to me. I couldn't help chuckling, even though I was so worried.

There was a faint echo from under the bed. Was that Bindweed laughing too?

I slipped out of bed and looked underneath it. I couldn't see anything because it was pitch dark, but I could hear the little chuckling sound . . . or was it *sobbing*?

'Bindweed?' I whispered and felt around in the dark. I touched the brocade of my slipper. I felt Bindweed's soft dress, her long strange curls, her tiny face. Her cheeks were wet.

'Oh, Bindweed, don't cry!' I said, scooping her into my hand.

She didn't resist. She just lay there limply, making small forlorn sobs. I wrapped my fingers round her and lifted her up into bed with me. I put her on my pillow and pulled my duvet up to her little chin.

'There now,' I said, giving her a gentle pat.

All the fight seemed to have gone out of her. She stayed still, though her body quivered every time she sobbed.

'Are you very unhappy?' I whispered.

I felt her nod.

'What can I do to make you feel better?' I asked.

She made a huge effort to speak instead of sob. 'Wentworth!' she murmured.

I knew she was going to say it. But it didn't seem as if she was simply being artful to get her own way. She seemed genuinely sad. I was suddenly frightened she might fade away altogether. Could fairies die of a broken heart?

I could feel my own heart thumping hard. It was bringing back those awful memories of Mum sobbing all the time when Dad had left us. She'd hardly seemed to know Robin and I were there. She'd cried and cried and we didn't know what to

do. It was the scariest time of my life. I had to tell someone, and then Mum got taken away to get help and we got taken away too. Our foster mum was really kind to us but we cried too because we wanted to go home so badly.

'I'll take you to Wentworth tomorrow, Bindweed,' I whispered. 'I promise I will.'

Bindweed still sobbed, but she reached out her arms and clasped my finger tight. After a few minutes her grip relaxed and she seemed to be asleep. I stayed awake, wondering how on earth I could take her there.

I must have fallen asleep at some point because I dreamed I was running through the Wentworth estate pursued by boys with toad faces and flippers for feet trying to smear me with slime. I woke with such a start that I woke Bindweed too.

'Mab?' she said hoarsely. She'd hurt her throat with all that crying.

'It's all right – I was only having a bad dream,' I said, shuddering.

'Are you still taking me to Wentworth?' she asked.

'Yes. I promised, didn't I?' I said.

And all of a sudden I knew how I was going to do it. It was such a daring plan that it shocked me. I'd always been such a

goodie-goodie. I was the sensible girl who looked after her mum and her little brother and was the teacher's pet at school. Now I was going to do something that even Micky Flynn would baulk at. If I could get away with it . . .

I could hear Mum going into the bathroom. Robin ran into my room and jumped into bed with me.

'I had the best dream ever, Mab! Fido turned into a real dog, but without his little wheels and the push-along bit. He could run all by himself and he kept leaping up and licking my knees, truly he did!' Robin said, bouncing about with excitement.

'Keep still, Robin!' I said urgently. Bindweed had scurried under my pillow and he was likely to squash her flat.

'No, let's play bouncy castles,' said Robin, standing up and jumping.

'Stop it!' I said. 'You're making me feel sick! Why don't you go and have a good peer at Fido, in case your dream's come true?'

Robin hurried off. I peered anxiously underneath my pillow. Bindweed was hunched in a ball, arms over her head.

'Was it an earthquake?' she groaned.

'No, just my little brother. Look, he'll only be gone a

minute. We'll have to be quick,' I said, leaping out of bed and fetching my school bag. 'Climb in!'

Bindweed looked inside the dark school bag. It was a jumble of notebooks and pencils and chocolate wrappers and a forgotten half-sandwich. I suppose it didn't look very inviting.

'I'm not going in there!' she protested.

'You'll have to! Look, I'll wrap you up in a sock so it's more comfy,' I said.

'A *sock*?' Bindweed sounded appalled.

'A clean one! Please hurry – you don't want Robin or Mum to see you, do you?' I said urgently.

'But why can't I simply pop back into the slipper under your bed?' Bindweed moaned.

'Because I'm taking you to school with me,' I whispered.

'To *school*?' Bindweed repeated, horrified. 'I can't go to your school! The other children would see me! And your teacher would think I was a butterfly and whack me with her cane!'

'I'm going to keep you totally hidden. And teachers don't have canes now, and even if they did Mrs Horsley would never ever whack you. She's lovely. She'd be totally in awe of you.'

'She'd keep me as a specimen under glass. I've heard tell

of several fairies enduring a living death in those exact circumstances,' Bindweed hissed.

'Look, you're just jolly well going to have to trust me,' I insisted. 'Do you want to go to Wentworth or not?'

'Of course I want to go to Wentworth,' said Bindweed.

'Well, this is the only way I can think of. All you have to do is stay in my school bag and keep quiet. OK?'

'What about my breakfast?'

'I'll see if I can find you something,' I said, getting a sock from my underwear box and wrapping it round her.

She fussed irritably and protested as I picked her up and put her into my school bag, but without as much vigour as before. I carried the bag over to the window and had a careful look at her in daylight. She really didn't look very well at all. Her head lolled wearily and her white face had purple marks under her eyes like tiny bruises. She wasn't acting to try to get me to take her to the Wentworth estate. She seemed really to be languishing. Frighteningly so. All those years hibernating in a book, and now I'd woken her up again, given her life – but for how long?

I left the school bag on my bed, carefully propped upright.

'I'll be back soon, Bindweed. Try to have a little nap,'

I whispered, giving the bag a pat, and then I hurried to get washed and dressed and have my breakfast.

Mum had brought a bashed packet of sugary cornflakes back from the supermarket. I poured myself a bowlful and slipped a few into my pocket too. Bindweed seemed to have a sweet tooth so she might like to crunch on them, as if they were giant pieces of sweet toast. I munched mine hurriedly and then, while Robin was still spooning his up, I went to look at the *Fairy Paintings* book again.

'I wouldn't look at that book too often – it'll give you nightmares,' said Mum. 'Though of course it was very kind of Mrs Horsley to give it to you.'

I flipped through the paintings, pausing only to give the golden-haired man a little prod with my finger. I turned the pages until I found the picture of the fairy's funeral. I stared at it, my heart beating fast. Bindweed looked as white and waxy as the poor dead fairy lying on the leaf, one hand on her stomach, the other hanging down uselessly.

'Mum, can fairies actually die?' I asked.

'Darling, don't!' said Mum, her eyes swivelling towards Robin. He wasn't taking any notice, simply shovelling in his cornflakes while humming a tune at the same time.

'But do they?' I persisted. 'I mean, there aren't many around now, are there? So they must have mostly died off.'

'I suppose their numbers have dwindled here . . . They must have all gone to Fairyland,' said Mum brightly. She hated to tell me anything upsetting.

'But they can die?' I said. I pointed to the picture. 'This shows a fairy's funeral, see.'

'Yes, but that's a very morbid painting. The fairy's pretty enough, but look at all those horrid red and yellow creatures with the googly eyes! Shut that book up quick, Mab,' said Mum, shuddering.

'No, I want to see the creatures with the googly eyes!' said Robin, cramming the last spoonful of cornflakes into his mouth, and then hiccupping.

'I wish you wouldn't bolt your food like that, sweetheart. And you don't want to see those nasty monsters,' said Mum.

'I do, I do!' said Robin.

'Put that book *away*, Mab,' said Mum.

I raised my eyebrows but stowed it back on the shelf obediently. Mum supervised Robin's teeth-cleaning while I whizzed into the bedroom and checked on Bindweed in my school bag. I gently eased her out of the sock.

'I've got you some lovely breakfast!' I said.

I would adore a sugary cornflake as big as a tea tray, but Bindweed didn't seem very interested. She took two nibbles and then passed it back to me. I don't think she liked the taste very much but she didn't complain. This worried me more than anything.

'You don't feel very well, do you, Bindweed?' I said.

It was her turn to raise her tiny eyebrows. 'I feel a little faint,' she murmured. 'But I'm sure I will revive when I see dear Wentworth.'

'Perhaps you've got dehydrated from all that crying?' I said.

I'd pocketed a little china thimble patterned with cheeky elves from the living-room mantelpiece. Bindweed pulled a face when she saw the picture, but drained the water gratefully, though it must have been like drinking direct from a bucket. It revived her a little, but not as much as I'd hoped.

I felt very anxious. It would be terrible if one of the last fairies in the country died because I didn't look after her properly. It would all be my fault. I wrapped Bindweed up in the sock again very tenderly and tucked her back at the top of my school bag.

'I promise I'm taking you to Wentworth today – only don't

blame me if you don't like it there any more,' I said.

'Mab? Who are you talking to?' Robin asked, running into my room. He had toothpaste froth all round his mouth.

'I'm not talking to anyone,' I said quickly, buckling the straps of my school bag.

'Yes you were! I heard you,' said Robin. He was staring at my bag. 'You were talking to something in there!'

'Oh! Well, promise not to tell,' I said.

I felt Bindweed scuttle in alarm to the bottom of the bag. I patted it to reassure her.

'I was just having a conversation with my mouse,' I said matter-of-factly.

'You haven't got a mouse,' said Robin.

'Not a real one. A pretend one,' I said. 'He's called Nibbles.'

'Can I see him?' Robin asked eagerly.

'There's nothing to see because he's pretend. I make him up. He keeps me company at school,' I said.

'Because you haven't got many friends?' said Robin.

I winced. 'I suppose so,' I said.

'Billie and those other girls are mean to you now, aren't they?' said Robin, and he came and gave me a hug. 'You can share my friends if you like.'

Robin's friends were all funny little kids who ran around the playground screeching like racing cars and laughing uproariously at fart jokes, but it was kind of him all the same.

'Thanks but no thanks,' I said, giving him a hug back. 'And you can share Nibbles – but don't tell anyone or they'll laugh at us.'

Robin mimed zipping his mouth and skipped off to find his own school bag. 'Maybe I'll have my own pretend mouse,' he called over his shoulder. 'I shall call her Munchy. She can

 126

be Nibbles' girlfriend. Then maybe they could have babies – that would be cool, wouldn't it?'

I bent and put my mouth to the flap of my school bag. 'It's all right, Bindweed,' I whispered. 'Robin just thinks you're a mouse.' I was proud of my quick thinking, but she was not impressed.

'It is not all right,' Bindweed replied faintly. 'I am *not* a mouse, a common field creature with a twitching nose and an ungainly scuttle. How dare you!'

At least it had roused her a little.

'I'm sorry. I didn't mean to insult you. I was only trying to protect you,' I said.

'Hmph!' said Bindweed. She paused. 'You will still take me to Wentworth, won't you?' she said more politely.

'I will,' I said firmly.

Although finding a real fairy had been the most amazing thing ever, she was proving such a trial that I was beginning to think it would be a relief to say goodbye to her.

CHAPTER EIGHT

I was very preoccupied on the way to school, plotting my great escape. When we got to the Infants gate, Robin went skipping off.

'Bye, Mum! Bye, Mab! Bye, Nibbles!' he cried.

'Nibbles?' Mum said to me.

'Oh, it's just a game. I pretended I had a pet mouse,' I said.

'You two!' said Mum. She was looking at me carefully as we went down the road to the Juniors. 'Have you got something on your mind, Mab?' she asked.

'No,' I said, which was probably the biggest lie I'd ever told.

'You look a bit worried, lovie,' said Mum. 'You would tell me if something was wrong, wouldn't you?'

'Yes, of course I would,' I said. Second biggest lie! Mum was looking so concerned, biting at the skin on her lip. '*You're* the one who looks worried, Mum.'

She sighed. 'I am a bit. That blooming Mr Henry's called a staff meeting before we open the shop today. Goodness knows what he's going to be moaning about now. He's making so many changes to the shop we don't know where we are.' Mum yawned. 'I'm scared he might change *me*!' She said it like a joke but I could tell she was serious.

'What do you mean, Mum?'

'He's always watching me, listening to the way I chat to the customers, especially the old lonely ones. Maybe he thinks I'm wasting time. I got so nervous yesterday I rang up the wrong item and had to start all over again. What if he thinks I'm a waste of space and gets rid of me?'

'Oh, Mum,' I said helplessly. 'Of course he won't.' I gave her a hug. 'I bet he thinks you're the best member of staff ever. If I was an old lady I'd choose your checkout every time because you're so nice.'

She gave me a big smile but she still looked worried.

She'd have been so much more worried if she knew what I was plotting.

Some of the Year Six boys were larking around in the playground playing football. Micky was playing too, though he was younger.

'Want to join in, Mab?' he called.

'What? We don't want some random little girly,' said Joey, Micky's big brother. 'It's bad enough putting up with you, squirt.'

'She's not random. She's an ace player,' said Micky. 'And she does ballet, so she's dead nimble on her feet.'

I was astonished. Joey looked amazed too.

'What? Oh, I get it! She's your girlfriend!' he said, spluttering with laughter. All the other boys joined in too.

Micky went as red as a tomato. 'Shut up, you lot. She's not my girlfriend. She's my mate,' he said. 'Come on, Mab, we'll play our own game of footie.'

I was truly touched. Micky Flynn wanted me to be his mate! We'd always been complete opposites. He was the bad boy, I was the goodie-goodie girl. We'd hardly spoken to each other before my birthday. But we seemed to get on together now. You knew where you were with Micky.

He didn't cosy up to you one minute and then go off with someone else the next.

'Yeah, let's play footie, Micky,' I said.

The only trouble was, we didn't have a ball.

'We could use your school bag,' Micky suggested. 'It's not round; it's kind of oval, but that doesn't matter. We'll play rugger.'

'Are you serious? No!' I said, clutching my bag.

'It's OK, I won't tackle you too hard,' said Micky.

'Use your own school bag!' I said. I could feel Bindweed scrabbling in terror. One kick from Micky could be fatal.

'Haven't got one any more,' said Micky. 'I kicked it into someone's garden by accident and it flattened all their prize dahlias and they wouldn't give it back. My nan won't buy me another one. She wanted me to use a manky old carrier bag – imagine! I'd be a laughing stock.'

'So where are all your pens and pencils and your packed lunch?'

'I'll borrow. And share,' said Micky.

'Is that why you suddenly want to be mates with me?' I said.

'No, it's because you're fun,' said Micky. 'Come on, let's

play!' He suddenly pushed my school bag right out of my arms and ran off with it.

'Don't you dare kick my bag!' I yelled, and I charged after him. He's a fast runner, but so am I, and I barged straight into him and grabbed the bag before he had a chance to kick it. I'm small and thin, but I hurtled at him full on, so he ended up flat on the ground.

'Hey! What did you do that for?' he said, starting to roll about, his face agonized. I hoped he was just acting, but I couldn't be sure.

'Are you OK?' I asked.

'No I'm not! Look at my knees! I'm bleeding!' Micky groaned.

I peered in terror. It was only a drop or two of blood, but it was enough to make me feel dreadful.

'Oh, Micky, I'm so sorry!' I said, squatting down beside him, cradling my school bag. I was desperate to peer inside to see if Bindweed was all right.

'I promised not to tackle you. I didn't expect you to tackle me!' Micky said. 'We'll have to start calling you Mab the Grab.'

'Stop it!'

'First you knock Cathy flying, and now it's my turn!' said Micky, scrambling to his feet.

'Shut *up*!' I knew he was only joking now, but it worried me all the same. And I was already worried enough. Bindweed didn't seem to be moving.

I started hurrying towards the school door.

'Hey! Wait for me! Forget playing footie. I've been spying on Joey and I'm pretty sure I've worked out the combination for his padlock. Let's go and see if we can ride his bike,' said Micky.

'He'll kill you if he sees you. And probably me too,' I said. 'No, I want to go into school.'

'What for? It's ages till the bell goes,' said Micky.

'I just do. I need to – to look something up. For my project,' I said.

'Boring!' said Micky. 'What are you doing your project on, eh?'

'It's a secret,' I said quickly. I hadn't made up my mind yet. I wasn't sure the Victorians were such a great idea after all. It might start to be too much like a history lesson. Mrs Horsley wanted something original. 'What are you doing for your project, Micky?' I asked.

I was sure he'd choose football, like most of the boys. Or maybe bikes. Or a video game?

'I'm doing spiders,' said Micky.

'Oh, ha ha,' I said sarcastically.

'I really am. I love spiders. I thought I'd collect a few too and bring them to school. That'll get all the girls squealing,' said Micky, chuckling.

'That's a rubbish sexist remark. I'm not the slightest bit scared of spiders,' I said. It was true. Mum squealed when she spotted a spider, and Robin made a big fuss too, but I could pick one up and put it gently out the window.

I wished I'd thought of choosing spiders for my project. It was a great idea. I was pretty certain Cathy would be frightened of spiders. I wondered how Bindweed would feel about them. I wasn't sure how I'd feel if a spider was almost as big as me.

'Anyway, got to go,' I said, running indoors.

'Little swot!' Micky called after me, but not in a really nasty way.

I hurried into the toilets, locked myself in a cubicle, sat on the loo and opened up my school bag. I peered inside anxiously. I couldn't see Bindweed for a moment and panicked – but then I spotted her right at the bottom, still inside my sock, just her green hair sticking out with her cap knocked sideways.

'Bindweed?' I whispered. 'No one can see you now. We're safe!'

'*Safe?*' Bindweed muttered bitterly. 'First I go whirling through the air, tumbled round and round until I don't know whether I'm up or down or sideways, and then the snatch-monster starts talking about the deadly enemy.'

'The what?'

'The arachnids!'

'The who?'

'*The-what the-who*! Is that your owl imitation?' Bindweed asked rudely. 'What is the point of going to school if they don't educate you? Spiders! The only good spider is an upside-down one with all eight legs in the air!'

'There's no need to be scared of spiders, Bindweed,' I said. 'There are very few poisonous ones in this country. They're mostly totally harmless, even the big ones.'

'Remind me of *that* when one of these totally harmless spiders is spinning a tight web round and round me until I can't move,' said Bindweed. 'I'll choke out, "Who's right now?" with my dying breath.'

'Oh. I see. Sorry! So what do you do if a spider comes scuttling along?' I asked.

'I like to keep a blackthorn spear to hand and then I spear the evil creature right between the eyes,' said Bindweed.

'That's a bit violent, isn't it?' I said. I was rather glad Bindweed was very tiny. I wouldn't reckon my chances if *she* were big and *I* was small.

I heard someone come into the toilets and put my finger to my lips. I pulled Bindweed's sock up round her neck, laid her down on top of my schoolbooks, and zipped up my bag. Then I flushed the loo and went outside.

I was washing my hands when Billie emerged from one of the cubicles.

We looked at each other, looked away quickly, and then looked back again sheepishly.

'Hi!' Billie murmured.

'Hi!' I said back. 'Thank you for the kitten book.'

'Oh. That's OK. I thought the little ones with the big blue eyes were so cute,' said Billie.

'Yes, they were,' I said, though I'd been so absorbed in the fairy book that I'd only glanced at Billie's present. 'Remember when we used to pretend *we* were cats?'

'Yeah. We went around miaowing all the time. We must have been totally bananas,' said Billie.

I shrugged. We both knew we'd adored playing the cat game. I was called Tiger and she was called Tiddles and we went scavenging every playtime. Sometimes the game seemed so real that she stopped being Billie altogether and actually seemed to have a cat face and a long tail.

She didn't ever play those kind of games with Cathy and Anita. They just went round and round the playground together with linked arms, talking to each other. Cathy did most of the chatting, and Billie and Anita nodded or giggled. It was sickening.

Billie washed her hands too, making them extra soapy. Then she blew a bubble. I did the same. Then we both blew lots of bubbles. This was another game we always played together, though once a cleaning lady caught us and told us off for wasting soap.

A little clump of younger girls came into the toilets and Billie looked up anxiously.

'It's OK, it's not Cathy,' I said.

Billie looked uncomfortable.

'How come you're OK when she's not around but you're mean to me when she is?' I asked. I was surprised. I was *thinking* that, but I hadn't meant to say it out loud.

'I'm not mean,' said Billie.

'Yes you are,' I said, looking her straight in the eyes.

'Well, you know what Cathy's like. You have to keep on the right side of her,' Billie mumbled.

'Why?' I persisted.

'Because she's Cathy,' Billie said.

'Well, I'm Mab. Why don't you want to stay on the right side of me?' I said.

'I do,' said Billie, but then Cathy and Anita really did come into the toilets. Billie leaped away from me and started rinsing her hands determinedly.

'Ugh! There's a terrible smell in here!' said Cathy, holding her nose.

Anita held her nose too.

The Year Three girls stared.

'Didn't you notice the stink, Billie?' Cathy asked pointedly. 'Why aren't you holding your nose?'

'My hands are wet,' said Billie. She shook them, spraying little droplets of water. Then, turning her back on me, she held her nose.

'*I* think there's a terrible rotten disgusting smell,' I said. 'But it only started reeking when *you* came into the toilets, Cathy.'

One of the Year Three girls burst out laughing and the others joined in. I swept out of the toilets clutching my school bag, feeling triumphant. My hands were still soapy but I didn't care. I wiped them on my skirt. They left white marks but at least they were clean marks.

I walked into the classroom, put my bag on my desk and unzipped it. 'Do you want to have a quick peek at my classroom, Bindweed?' I whispered.

Bindweed struggled upwards. The sock had wound itself round her too tightly now and I had to help her. She peered round. Mrs Horsley's classroom was the nicest in the whole school. Whenever a visitor came, they were always shown our room because it was so colourful, with pictures all over the walls.

'That's one of my paintings over there, the one with the fair lady and the little boy and the girl. That's my family portrait,' I said. 'My teacher Mrs Horsley said it was ever so good.'

'My family were painted for a portrait once, in the finest of details,' said Bindweed, clearly thinking my own painting a mere daub.

She didn't seem to think much of our clay animals either, or the papier mâché puppets hanging from the ceiling, or the life-sized Egyptian mummy that we'd all had a turn at painting. She shuddered at the bright bookshelves.

'You won't trap me inside one of those books, will you?'

'Of course not,' I said.

The only thing she approved of was the vase of flowers

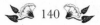

from Mrs Horsley's garden. She stared at the roses, inhaling so deeply that her tiny nostrils quivered.

'Oh, such sweet perfume! My kinfolk and I loved to bind ourselves to those heavenly roses at Wentworth,' she said. 'Can't we go there now?'

'I'm *taking* you. But I have to get registered first or Mrs Horsley will wonder where I am. She might even contact Mum. But I'm going to give her the slip. You'll see.'

The school bell suddenly rang. Bindweed shrieked and covered her ears.

'It's OK, it only means school's starting. Better bob back in the bag again before they all start trooping in,' I said.

Cathy and Anita held their noses when they pushed past my desk. Billie put her hand up to do it too, but when she saw me looking she rubbed her nose with the back of her hand as if she just had an itch. Micky came in several minutes after all the others, when Mrs Horsley was starting to take the register. She frowned at him and gestured to him to sit down quickly.

He lounged against my desk instead. 'You missed out big time, Mab! I got Joey's bike unpadlocked easy-peasy and once he went into school I rode the whole way round the playground.

You could have had a turn too!' he whispered.

'Micky Flynn, stop gossiping and sit down at once!' said Mrs Horsley.

'Sorry, miss,' said Micky cheerfully, and swaggered off to his own desk.

I was a little bit envious because I'd always longed to try a proper mountain bike, but maybe I'd get a chance another day. Meanwhile I had to concentrate on my cunning plan.

We had maths and English for the first two lessons. They seemed to go on for six years at least, and I heard little moans and sighs coming from my school bag – but at last the bell rang again for playtime. I grabbed the bag and ran for it, while most of the class were still dawdling around.

Most of the class.

'Hey, wait for me, Mab!' It was Micky Flynn, thudding along beside me.

'Oh, Micky! Look, I'm sorry, I can't hang about,' I said hurriedly.

'Don't be daft! You're heading for the bike sheds, aren't you? It might be a bit dodgy getting on Joey's bike right now, when everyone's milling about the playground, but we can give it a go if you like,' said Micky, keeping pace with me now.

'I'm not going to the bike sheds,' I puffed.

'Yes you are!' he protested.

'I'm going *behind* the bike sheds,' I said. 'Now do clear off, Micky, please!'

'What are you going to do behind the sheds?' Micky asked. 'There's nothing there – just a scrubby bit of grass and the fence. What are you up to, eh?'

It was no use trying to shake him off.

'Look, Micky, will you swear not to tell on me?' I asked.

'Course I won't. I'm your mate, aren't I?'

'OK then. I'm bunking off!' I said.

Micky's eyes went round. 'But you're Miss Goodie-Goodie.'

'Well, I'm Miss Baddie-Baddie today,' I said.

'Is it because those girls are so mean to you? Cathy and her henchmen?'

'No, I've got to go and do something,' I said. 'I can't tell you what. I've *got* to do it.'

'Hey, are you in real trouble, Mab?' Micky looked concerned. 'I'm coming with you!'

'No, you can't. This is something private. And if the two of us disappear then someone's bound to notice. But it's double PE with Mr Masters till lunchtime, and I'm hoping I'll be

back in time for afternoon registration.'

'You'll go without lunch?' said Micky.

'If I have to,' I said.

'Here!' He felt in his trouser pocket and brought out a chocolate biscuit. He took one bite and then handed the rest to me. 'You have it. And don't worry, I won't tell. I'll cover for you. I hope it goes OK. I think I've twigged what you're up to.'

I was pretty sure he hadn't. It wasn't the likeliest thing in the world, to be going to the most terrifying estate in town to release a small, bad-tempered fairy. I had no idea what he thought I was doing, but it didn't really matter.

'Thanks . . . mate,' I said. It sounded a bit silly, like I was an old man, but he grinned at me.

Then I dodged behind the bike sheds, hitched my bag over my shoulders, and leaped for the top of the fence. The wood cut in hard on my soft palms, but I still managed to press myself up, get one leg up and over, and then the other. I jumped for it and landed clumsily but safely on the other side. I heard Micky cheering softly as I started running again.

I ran in the wrong direction at first, because I didn't want to go past the front of the school. The staffroom was on the first floor and looked out over the school gate. I couldn't risk

Mrs Horsley idly glancing out the window as she sipped her cup of coffee. She had eyes like a hawk.

I did a long loop around the back streets and was completely out of breath by the time I got to the main road again. I had to lean on a wall to recover. Buses and cars and lorries thundered past. I heard faint groans coming from my school bag, and when an ambulance shrieked its way through the traffic there was frantic burrowing in the bag as Bindweed tried to bury herself in its depths, appalled by the noise.

I hurried along the road towards the big shopping centre where the streets were pedestrianized. I dawdled for just a moment outside a bicycle shop, peering at the mountain bikes. And the electric scooters! I wondered if Bindweed would be so grateful to me for taking her to Wentworth that she'd grant me a wish. A magic little fish in one fairy story granted an old fisherman a palace with gleaming golden thrones for him and his wife. I was quite happy to stay in our housing association flat. All I wanted was an electric scooter, but a bike would do, preferably a mountain one. It didn't have to be gold, it didn't have to be gleaming. A second-hand one off eBay would be fine.

My bag started shaking. Bindweed was jumping up and down impatiently. She didn't seem to be in the mood for

granting wishes. She was more a casting-evil-spells type of fairy. I knew I had to get her to the Wentworth estate as fast as possible or I might find donkey's ears sprouting out of my head or a wart as big as a boiled egg throbbing at the end of my nose.

It didn't do to loiter anyway as several people were staring at me curiously, clearly wondering what I was doing going round the shops by myself instead of being in school. They might approach me any second and enquire. I quickly clasped my cheek, grimaced and walked on purposefully, as if I had an urgent dental appointment.

I went out the other side of the shopping centre, down several streets of semis, on and on, my too-small trainers painfully squashing my toes. By the time I was approaching the Wentworth estate up the hill, I was limping.

'We're nearly there,' I said, talking into my school bag. I felt a flutter inside and the sound of small hands clapping.

I was in a flutter myself, but not with joy. The Wentworth estate looked bigger and bleaker than ever, its tall towers casting shadows over the piles of rubbish and burnt-out cars, and I couldn't help but remember all the stories I'd been told about the place. Luckily there was hardly anyone about, just a mother with a ponytail and fierce eyebrows pushing a

screaming baby in a buggy, and an old lady with a cardie over her nightie slowly making her way along the tarmac with a Zimmer frame.

I breathed a sigh of relief. Neither were likely to beat me up. I supposed most people were out at work or at school. I couldn't see any gangs of wild teenagers, thank goodness. If there really were any and they were as scary as some people said, they were probably still fast asleep in bed after a night out getting up to no good. What would happen if anyone horrible spotted Bindweed? One stamp of their boot and she'd be finished. And there were no gardens anywhere, so why she wanted to live here was a mystery.

I looked around and around for somewhere relatively private where I could release her. I tried a stairwell, but it smelled as if someone used it as a toilet. In the end I went up to the top floor of the nearest block so Bindweed could peep out and direct me to her favourite place. The lift wasn't working, so I had to walk up the steps. Up and up and up. It felt as if I'd gone right up above the clouds by the time I emerged on the top balcony.

I sat down on someone's rubber doormat and undid my school bag.

'We're here,' I whispered inside. 'It's safe to come out now.'

Nothing happened.

'Bindweed?' I said anxiously.

Still nothing.

I reached down into the bag and gently lifted her to the top, still inside the sock. She was lying motionless, eyes closed, face pearly white. For a terrible moment I thought she was dead, but then she sighed and opened her eyes.

'I feel so sick,' she murmured, and then turned her head and actually *was* sick, vomiting strange greeny liquid down onto my school books, pens and pencils, and Micky's chocolate biscuit. I was particularly sad about the biscuit because I was starving after my long walk and great climb upwards.

'Oh dear, poor Bindweed,' I said. 'I suppose you've been travel sick.'

'You've taken me up and up and up,' Bindweed groaned weakly. 'I feel so dizzy!'

'Try breathing deeply,' I suggested.

'I have altitude sickness, you foolish girl. I'm barely capable of drawing breath,' Bindweed snapped.

She peeled off the sock and climbed out of the bag – and then shrieked as a flock of birds flew past.

'Are we *up a tree*?' she gasped. 'Hide me from those winged monsters!'

'They're not fierce birds. They're only those black ones with little shiny bits,' I said. 'They're completely harmless.'

'Tell that to all the worms they peck!' said Bindweed, scrambling up to my shoulders. 'All birds are enemies to fairies. Especially starlings!' She squeezed inside the neck of my blouse until only her head stuck out. She was a little soggy now but I tried not to mind.

'Anyway, we're not up a tree. We're at the top of a block of flats, so you can see out,' I said.

'This is not a flat. This is an immensely high,' said Bindweed. 'Where *is* this bleak and dreadful place?'

'It's the Wentworth estate,' I said.

'Don't be ridiculous! How dare you mock me like this! I thought you were a kind, obedient girl,' Bindweed said furiously.

'I *am*! I've done exactly what you asked me to do. And if anyone finds out at school, I'll be in terrible trouble and they'll tell Mum and then she'll start worrying and might even get ill like she did before, and Robin and I will get taken away again,' I said, and the panic started up again. I found I was shaking

and couldn't stop, even though I clenched my fists and willed myself to calm down.

Bindweed was momentarily distracted by my state.

'There now,' she said, and she patted me with her tiny hand. 'I don't know why you're so distressed but I'm sure you have nothing to worry about. *I'm* the one who should be distraught. I want to go back to my dear leafy Wentworth, please – not this ugly, derelict nightmare without even a blade of grass.'

'But I absolutely promise you, this *is* Wentworth. I think it just looks different because we're so high up. We'll go down to the ground again and then you'll maybe recognize it,' I said, calming down a little. I hadn't had a panic like that for a long time and it frightened me. I wanted to forget all about this ridiculous rehoming mission and rush back to school straight away before anyone realized I was missing. Well, Micky knew – but I trusted him. I knew he'd never tell on me. It was funny. Billie had been my best friend ever since I came to this school but I'd never been absolutely certain she wouldn't tell all my secrets. And I'd been right.

I sighed. Bindweed sighed too. 'This is definitely not not not Wentworth. But do let's descend. It's making me feel extremely giddy.'

'Hop back in the bag then,' I said.

'Absolutely not!' said Bindweed in horror. 'It is polluted now!'

She was the one responsible for the polluting, and fairy sick didn't really smell very strongly, but I suppose I wouldn't have wanted to ride in a bag full of sick either. I didn't quite know how I was going to clean it all up, but I would face that problem later. I tucked her into my collar and then we went all the way down the stairs again. It took for ever. It felt as if we might reach Australia any minute. I hoped the old lady in her nightie with the Zimmer frame lived on the ground floor. And how would the mum with the ponytail and the baby in the buggy manage all these stairs?

When we were down on the ground again I walked right round the estate, my heart thudding. Even Micky would never dare stroll casually into Wentworth. My school uniform marked me out as a stranger too. I was like a moving target.

'I don't like it here!' Bindweed said underneath my chin.

'Neither do I,' I said.

'This must be a mistake. This *isn't* Wentworth!' Bindweed insisted.

'Oh yes it is!' I said. It sounded as if we were taking part in a pantomime.

The old lady in the nightie was still creeping along. She turned at the sound of my voice. 'Were you talking to me, dear?' she asked. 'You'll have to speak up. I'm a bit deaf nowadays.'

'I was just wondering if this is the Wentworth estate,' I said.

'Well, it's not Buckingham Palace, is it?' she said, cackling.

'So it definitely *is* the Wentworth estate,' I went on.

'The one and only,' she said. 'I've been living here since I was a kiddie, when it was built.'

I could see she was very old, but she couldn't possibly have been born way back in the Victorian age. She saw me looking puzzled and shook her head at me.

'It wasn't always an estate like this,' she said. 'Wentworth used to be a beautiful big country house, famous for its gardens. My granny used to go there when the garden was open to the public, and she said there were so many roses the smell made you dizzy.'

'Yes!' Bindweed burst out.

She spoke in the tiniest voice, but the old lady nodded her head as if she could hear her in spite of her deafness.

'Pink roses, white roses, yellow roses – but she said the best were the deep red roses,' the old lady mused.

Bindweed nodded emphatically, her ringlets tickling my neck.

I couldn't help looking around, wondering if a single rose bush might remain, but it was all asphalt and concrete everywhere. There weren't even any weeds.

'You won't see any here now, girlie!' the old lady chuckled. 'The soldiers lived here for a bit in the war, and then the house went to rack and ruin. So they knocked it down and bulldozed the grounds and built the estate.'

'How dreadful!' I said.

'But it was lovely in the beginning. Very smart. And all the folk who'd been living in grimy terraces with no hot water and toilets in the back yard thought it was their idea of heaven. But it's a dump now, I grant you. Still, it's home to me. They want me to go into an old folks' home since I broke my hip but I'm not having it. There's no place like home – your *real* home.'

She crept forward, hunched over her Zimmer frame, *step tap, step tap*, painfully slowly.

'Can I – can I help in any way?' I asked.

'I'm fine, dearie,' she said. 'Just taking my exercise. I'll do a star jump in a second. Ha!'

'What a lovely old lady,' I whispered to Bindweed.

She wasn't listening. She had cast herself down on my shoulder.

'There's no place like home,' she repeated brokenly. 'But I haven't got a home any more.' She gave a little tearful sniff. 'Where are my people? Am I alone? Where do all the fairy folk live now?'

'I'm so sorry. I didn't realize it used to be different. I couldn't understand why on earth you wanted to live here again. So . . . what shall we do now?'

'I don't know!' Bindweed said and started sobbing.

CHAPTER NINE

I didn't know where to take Bindweed. The nearby streets had houses with little gardens, but some had been concreted over to make space for a car, and the gardens that were left weren't very picturesque. I couldn't spot a rose bush anywhere. I couldn't simply abandon her in a patch of grass and hope for the best. Besides, I had to get back to school before I was found out.

'Don't worry. I'll find you a lovely new home – I promise. But right now you'll have to come back to school with me or I shall get into terrible trouble.'

'I don't like your school!' Bindweed wailed.

'I don't like it very much either, but I have to go. That's the rule,' I said.

'I am so glad I am me and not you. Fairies delight in breaking the rules. We don't plod along dully doing things we don't want to do,' said Bindweed.

'I don't *plod*. I ran like the wind to get out of school. And I'm not *dull*. I'm very daring. No one else would bunk off school and go to the Wentworth estate!' I said hotly. 'Now just stop your moaning and come with me.'

I wasn't cross enough to stuff her back in the school bag. I couldn't run properly with Bindweed down my neck because she was half choking me. In the end I stuffed her down one of the socks I was wearing and set off. She clasped me round my ankle bone and moaned that she was feeling dizzy as I sped along.

'I can't win. You sneer at me for plodding and whine when I go fast. I've got to hurry. I can't miss afternoon registration!' I panted.

In actual fact I got back in the middle of lunchtime. I was able to grab a slice of pizza and an apple. I slipped a little morsel of both into my sock under cover of the table so that Bindweed had lunch too. Billie and Anita and Cathy

were right over the other side of the dining hall, taking no notice of me. Micky was too, but he waved when he spotted me, and came charging over, stuffing a banana down his throat.

'Micky Flynn! Will you sit down until you've actually finished your lunch!' said a dinner lady. 'You'll give yourself terrible hiccups.'

'Got them already, miss,' said Micky cheerfully, and hiccupped loudly to demonstrate. He sat down beside me. 'No one noticed you were missing!' he said. 'Well, Cathy asked where you'd got to, and I said – *hic* – you'd felt sick and had to go to the toilets, so that shut her up – *hic*.'

'Thanks,' I said. 'Drink a glass of water from the wrong side and it'll cure your hiccups.'

He tried with a lot of spluttering, and several *hics*, but by the time he'd got to the bottom of the glass it had worked.

'Hey, you're magic, Mab!' he said. He lowered his voice. 'So where did you really go, eh?'

'I went for a stroll round the Wentworth estate,' I said.

'Oh, ha ha!' said Micky. 'Where did you really go? I won't tell, I swear. I bet you went to meet your dad!'

I stared at him in astonishment. 'No I didn't!'

'It's OK. I get it. Me and my brother sometimes see my mum and her new boyfriend in secret. We don't let on to Nan because it upsets her. She's scared we'll go off and live with Mum and some stepdad. As if!' said Micky.

'Well, I haven't got a stepdad, and I won't ever have one because Mum still hopes our dad will come back, though that isn't going to happen in a million years,' I said, sighing.

'But you'd like it if he did, eh?'

'No I wouldn't. He made my mum very unhappy,' I said. 'But Mum wants him back.'

'What about you? Don't you miss him?' Micky asked curiously.

'Not one bit. I couldn't care less about him,' I said. This was a really big lie, and it worried me. I couldn't cross my fingers because Micky would see. I crossed my ankles instead.

There was a small scream from the regions of my sock.

'What was that?' said Micky, his nose wrinkling.

'I didn't hear anything,' I lied again.

'Do you think it was a mouse squeaking?' said Micky. He peered under the table before I could stop him but Bindweed dived further down my sock, out of sight. If she could do that, it meant I hadn't hurt her too badly.

'Let's go round the bike sheds then,' said Micky. 'Have you ever tried out a mountain bike?'

I hadn't ever ridden *any* kind of bike, apart from a toddler trike when I was about two. But I knew I'd just sit on the saddle, grasp the handlebars and start pedalling – and I'd be off, practically flying down the road, everyone taken aback by my style and speed. Marvel Mab, champion biker!

But there was no chance of living out my fantasy, because Micky's brother Joey was there himself with one of his mates, and they were using the side of the bike sheds to play kick-the-ball. Then my own brother came rushing up.

'*There* you are, Mab! I've been looking everywhere for you!' he said, flinging his arms round my waist.

'Oh, Robin, don't be such a little wuss,' I said, but I hugged him back hard, feeling guilty.

'What's a wuss?' he asked.

'It's a little softie squirt like you,' said Micky. 'I'm going to have to teach you to be tough like me. Want to learn to box? Put your fists up!'

'He's too young to box! Don't you dare hit him!' I said – but Micky winked at me. He just danced round Robin, and Robin danced too, and Micky dabbed at his chest and head

and bent down to let Robin do the same to him. Then Micky pretended Robin had won the first round and raised his arms in the air and called him a champion.

'You're brilliant with Robin, Micky,' I said, when we went into school. 'He loved you boxing with him.'

'I'll teach *you* to box if you like. Then you can knock Cathy flying,' he said.

'Her mum would go bonkers if I did,' I said, though the thought was glorious.

Cathy held her nose as I went into the classroom, and Anita did too – and Billie.

'What's that awful smell?' said Cathy.

Micky took a big sniff and then doubled up, nose wrinkled, tongue hanging out at the side of his mouth, a cartoon of disgust. 'Eeeewww!' he said. 'It's Catty Cathy and she's just made the yuckiest smell ever!'

All the boys started laughing, and even some of the girls. Then Mrs Horsley came into the classroom.

'That's what I like to see – happy smiling faces!' she said. 'Now let's settle down for our art lesson. You painted some lovely landscapes last time. Let's check – does everyone remember what a landscape is?'

'Yes, Mrs Horsley. I've got a phone so I know it's when you take a photo of something sideways with it,' said Cathy. Her face was still red with fury and humiliation, but she couldn't miss this chance of pointing out that she had her own smart-phone. We weren't allowed to take phones to school, but Cathy often did.

'You're quite right, Cathy. Taking a photo sideways is indeed called landscape. And portraits are taller up than across. But photographs are very different from paintings. Can anyone tell me why?'

'Photos can make you laugh, Mrs Horsley – like videos. I like funny cats on YouTube,' said Billie.

'That's true,' said Mrs Horsley.

'Photos are better because they show what things are really like,' said Anita.

'Especially if you've got a great camera,' said Cathy.

'Sometimes paintings can make you *feel* more, though,' said Mrs Horsley. 'A great artist can paint things in such a way that you feel happy or so moved that your heart starts thumping. What do we call these feelings?'

'Acting soft, miss,' said Micky.

Mrs Horsley sighed. 'They're emotions, Micky.

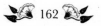

Now, remember Van Gogh's painting of a yellow cornfield and Monet's bright poppies?' She pointed to the pictures pinned on the wall. 'How do they make you feel?'

They didn't make me feel particularly happy, especially with the problem of a home for Bindweed looming large, but I knew the answer she was hoping for.

'Happy, Mrs Horsley,' I said.

'Exactly! Well done, Mab,' said Mrs Horsley. 'They might not be exact reproductions of real cornfields and poppies, but they're somehow better, because they make us feel glad to look at them. Lovely vibrant colours. Now, how do you feel when you look at *this* painting?' she asked, this time showing us a painting of a lady in a white dress, fast asleep with a horrible gargoyle creature crouching on her tummy in the gloomy darkness. 'This is called *The Nightmare* by a painter called Henry Fuseli. So it makes you feel . . . ?'

'Frightened,' we chorused, apart from Micky, who squatted on his chair and pulled a horrible gargoyle face in imitation.

'That's enough, Micky,' said Mrs Horsley wearily. 'Right, everyone: time to paint some pictures! Landscape, portrait – whatever you fancy. But I want to see if you can convey some

kind of emotion with your choice of colour. Show me how you are feeling today.'

She handed out sheets of paper and told us to choose our paints. There was a big rush to grab the yellow and red pots. I didn't care. I took a pot of white and a pot of black. I'd decided to try a cityscape, and as long as I had black and white to make different shades of grey I was happy.

Bindweed seemed bored by this lesson and was very still, probably asleep, which was a relief.

'What's that you're painting?' Micky asked, craning over to see.

'It's the Wentworth estate,' I said, carefully painting grey slabs of concrete.

'You're so weird,' said Micky.

He couldn't make up his mind whether to do a yellow cornfield or red poppies, so he did both, sloshing the yellow paint on liberally and then dotting in lots of red flowers. He didn't wait for the paint to dry properly, so the red ran all over the paper, making it look as if there had been a terrible slaughter in the cornfield.

'Oh well. It's like one of those modern paintings where it's all splashes,' said Micky. He looked a bit like a painting himself,

with yellow on his sleeves and the tip of his nose and red all over his fingers.

Mrs Horsley sighed at him when she came round to look at our paintings.

'I should have a good scrub before you go home, Micky,' she said. 'Still, it looks as if you've been enjoying yourself.'

She looked worried when she saw my own painting, though I'd done it as carefully as I could. I'd even made a special dark shade of grey for the shadows. I painted the people grey too – a mum with a pushchair and an old lady with a Zimmer frame at opposite ends of the picture.

'You've painted your landscape beautifully, Mab. Well done. It's very effective. It does all look very bleak,' she said. Mrs Horsley had obviously never been round the Wentworth estate. 'Perhaps you could put a few dabs of colour here and there? Maybe several of the flats could have bright curtains? And there could be a little girl like you skipping along the path between the buildings. Bring in some happy feelings too. I know, you could make a little garden in this corner here, with bright green grass and lots of pretty flowers,' she suggested.

'Flowers!' a small voice echoed longingly from the floor. Bindweed had obviously woken up.

Luckily I had my hand over my mouth so Mrs Horsley thought it was me.

'That's right,' she said. 'Otherwise it is such a sad painting.' She paused, still looking worried. She bent down beside me and said very softly, 'Do *you* feel really sad, Mab?'

I thought about it. I always felt a bit worried about Mum, and angry about Dad, and upset that Billie didn't want to be my friend any more, and now I had this new and pressing problem about rehoming a fairy – but I didn't feel *sad* exactly.

'No, I'm fine, Mrs Horsley,' I said as brightly as I could. 'But I'll try to make my picture more cheerful.'

It was actually good fun adding little dabs of colour here and there. I gave the mum a smiley face and added a small boy like Robin, skipping along beside her in his favourite red hoodie like Little Red Riding Hood. I painted a goofy-looking me in a yellow T-shirt and blue jeans chatting to the old lady with the Zimmer frame, and I turned her faded nightie into a long dress patterned with flowers. I made a garden too and painted it with roses. I gave the biggest rose a little splodge of white that could just be a fairy. I wished it was possible to make everything as bright and happy in real life.

I was really pleased when Mrs Horsley held up my picture

for the whole class to see at the end of the art lesson.

'Teacher's pet,' Micky mocked predictably, but he clapped me on the back. 'Well done, though! You aren't half artistic!'

'I don't think it's that great,' said Cathy, when Mrs Horsley was busy putting all the paintbrushes in the sink. 'I think it looks stupid. Don't you, Anita?'

'Yeah, it looks kind of rubbish,' said Anita.

'What do you think, Billie?' Cathy asked.

Billie sniffed. She shrugged. 'I suppose,' she muttered.

'You suppose what?' Cathy asked.

Billie glanced at me. She bit her lip.

'You don't *like* it, do you?' Cathy continued.

'No! No, it's not my sort of thing at all,' said Billie. 'I mean, it's quite well-painted but –'

'No it's not! It's horrible,' said Cathy, and she gave Billie a sharp nudge. 'Isn't it?'

'No. I mean, yes! Whatever,' said Billie.

'What do you mean, "whatever"?' Cathy demanded.

'I think it looks awful,' said Billie, giving in.

I drooped in my chair. Why couldn't Billie stick up for me just once? We used to love drawing together at playtimes. She always begged me to do the heads of her girls because she said

I could do them much better than she could. She often said I was heaps better at art than she was.

I knew she was only saying my painting was awful to keep in with Cathy, but it still hurt.

My ankle prickled. My sock was being pulled this way and that. Bindweed was climbing out of it! I panicked and bent down to stuff her back in but she was too quick for me. She jumped down to the floor and scuttled forward before I could stop her. I stared as she made her way round chair legs and hurdled over feet. What was she *playing* at? Someone could so easily spot her if they glanced down. They might think she was a green-and-white spider and scream – or stamp on her!

'Mab? Are you all right, dear?' Mrs Horsley called from the front of the class.

I had to straighten up, the blood throbbing in my head.

'Yes, Mrs Horsley, I was just –'

'Just?' she said, her head on one side.

'Scratching my leg,' I added lamely.

Cathy giggled. 'Searching for fleas!' she said, barely lowering her voice.

Anita giggled too. And Billie.

Mrs Horsley frowned. 'Don't be silly, girls. Settle down now.'

I couldn't settle. Bindweed seemed to be making her way towards Cathy! I felt a moment of deep despair. Was she going to leave me and make friends with Cathy too? I had one more glance. She'd actually reached Cathy's snow-white designer trainers. Was she about to climb up her leg and beg to be *her* fairy?

'Mab!' Mrs Horsley was starting to be irritated now. 'Do sit up straight!'

I just had time to see that Bindweed was stealthily undoing the laces in Cathy's dazzling trainers! I sat upright, wondering what on earth she was doing.

'Now, I'd like to discuss your projects with you,' said Mrs Horsley. 'You've had a little time to think about it, and I hope

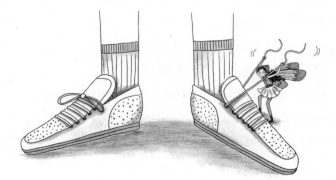

you've all decided what you want to do. I'm going to give out the special project notebooks now so you can take them home for the weekend and make a start.'

'Is that homework, miss?' Micky asked, sounding horrified. 'I didn't think we had to do any homework in our year.'

'It's not homework, Micky. It's project work – some of which you might care to do at home. There's a subtle difference,' said Mrs Horsley. 'Right, you can start the ball rolling. What is your project going to be about?'

'Spiders, miss,' said Micky.

There was a chorus of *ewws* and *yucks* but Mrs Horsley actually smiled.

'A very good idea, Micky! Well done. So what are you going to write about spiders?' she asked.

'Well. The different sorts. Especially tarantulas – they're the best. I could try drawing one, I suppose, but as you know I'm not that great at art, so I'll download a picture instead and print it out,' he said.

'That will be a good start. But I shall want you to expand your ideas considerably. Maybe you could write about the way many people react to spiders? And see if you can find out how they make their webs. You could find examples of spiders in

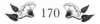

storybooks and art and films. There's so much you could write about,' said Mrs Horsley.

'A bit too much if you ask me!' said Micky.

'And I *do* ask you, Micky, because I am your teacher and you are supposed to follow my suggestions with good grace,' said Mrs Horsley.

'Yes, miss,' said Micky, knowing when he was defeated.

'Now, Billie, what are you going to do for your project?' Mrs Horsley asked.

'Cats, miss,' said Billie.

'No you're not,' said Cathy. 'We're going to work on a joint project about dance: you and me and Anita. I'm going to do ballet, Mrs Horsley, because I go to lessons and I'm always picked for the lead role. I don't want to boast, but I'm the best! Anita can do Indian dancing because she knows all about it, and Billie can do ballroom because she likes *Strictly*.'

'Yes, but I like cats more,' said Billie. 'Couldn't we do a joint project on cats?'

'I'm allergic to cats – you know I am. And I don't even like them. Dogs are much more fun,' said Cathy.

There was an immediate heated argument all around the

classroom, cat people versus dog people. I liked both but was too concerned about Bindweed to take part.

Mrs Horsley clapped her hands. 'Settle down, everyone! We're discussing projects, not having a debate about cats and dogs. Billie, I think a cat project is a splendid idea. You're obviously very interested in them.'

'I am. I know all about cats. And kittens.' Billie suddenly looked stricken. 'Oh no! I've given my kitten book to someone else.' She looked in my direction.

'I'll give it back – don't worry,' I mouthed at her, and she looked relieved.

'Perhaps you can write about the history of cats too. Did you know that the ancient Egyptians used to worship cats?' said Mrs Horsley.

'Oh, I've seen a cat mummy in the British Museum – my dad took me,' said Anita. 'Could I write about the ancient Egyptians for my project, Mrs Horsley?'

'Of course you can. I hope you draw me lots of mummies. And pyramids,' said Mrs Horsley.

'Well, *I'm* still doing a project on dancing,' said Cathy, very much in a huff. 'I'll do lots of drawings of ballet dancers. I can even stick in photos of me at dancing displays – my mum

always takes heaps. And I tell you what, I could actually do a demonstration. I can do pirouettes, six at a time without losing my balance once. Look!'

She stood up, held her head high, her arms spread. But before she danced a single step, she went crashing to the floor, landing on her bottom.

'Very graceful!' said Micky, and the whole class burst out laughing.

'Cathy! Oh dear, are you all right?' Mrs Horsley cried, rushing to pick her up. 'Goodness, you've got your trainer laces all tangled together! No wonder you fell over!'

'Someone's tied them up deliberately to make a fool of me!' Cathy roared. 'And I know who! It's Mab! She keeps bullying me, just because Billie wants to be my friend now.'

'Now calm down, Cathy,' said Mrs Horsley, checking her over for bumps and bruises. 'I know you're very upset but you mustn't make silly accusations. How could Mab have possibly tampered with your shoes? She sits three tables behind you!'

'She was bending down earlier. She could have reached out and done it,' Cathy insisted.

'Mab hasn't got six-metre-long arms, you twerp!' said Micky.

'Then you did it, Micky Flynn!' said Cathy.

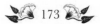

'I've been sitting here all lesson!' said Micky. 'How could I have done it?'

'Well, *someone* did!' Cathy spluttered, nearly in tears.

I knew who the someone was! She had scuttled back to my sock now and was hopefully completely hidden. I could hear tiny peals of laughter.

'What's that funny little noise?' asked Micky, who had very sharp ears.

'Sorry! It was me!' I whispered quickly. 'I couldn't help it. Cathy looked so funny.'

Bindweed had played a trick on Cathy because she'd been so sneery about my painting! She didn't want to be her friend. She was *my* friend – a very special friend – so Cathy was her enemy.

'I'm telling my mum!' said Cathy.

'There's nothing to tell, dear,' said Mrs Horsley briskly. 'You simply took a little tumble because your shoelaces got tangled. When you've done your dancing project you can wear your ballet shoes to demonstrate your lovely pirouettes. Now, who's next?'

Victoria put up her hand. She's the cleverest in our class. She's quite a nice girl, but very earnest.

'I'd love to do a project on the Victorians, Mrs Horsley,' she said. Her eyes shone behind her glasses. 'I want to write about Queen Victoria herself, and the life of very rich people with lots of servants, and I'm going to compare their lives with very poor people begging in the streets without enough to eat. I thought I'd write it as if I'm an interviewer going back in time, asking them all sorts of questions.'

'That's a splendid idea, Victoria. And very appropriate, given your name!' said Mrs Horsley.

It *was* a splendid idea. The trouble was, it had been my idea too, though I hadn't got as far as planning it because I'd been so busy with Bindweed. I wished I'd thought about it a bit harder.

Mrs Horsley was looking straight at me now.

'What's your project going to be, Mab?' she asked.

I hesitated. It would sound as if I were copying Victoria if I said I wanted to do a project on the Victorians too. I couldn't even think about an original way of presenting it. I tried to think of another good subject for a project. It was hopeless. Bindweed was still distracting me. She was poking me now with her little fingers, sharp as pins.

'Speak up, Mab,' Mrs Horsley prompted.

'She can't think of anything!' said Cathy, sniffing. She smiled spitefully. '*I* know what you can choose. Fairies! And you can dress up in that rubbish fairy outfit of yours!'

The class looked stunned, and then started sniggering.

'Yes!' said a tiny voice at my ankle.

'*Yes?*' said Micky.

I took a deep breath. 'Yes!' I said. 'That's a great idea, Cathy. I know quite a bit about them already, but I shall try to find out more. I shall do a project on fairies!'

CHAPTER TEN

'Are you nuts?' Micky asked, at the end of school.

'Probably,' I said.

'They'll all laugh at you if you start spouting about *fairies*,' said Micky.

'Then they'll be stupid. Fairies take offence very easily. They might find *their* laces get tied together so that they fall over,' I said.

'You're talking like you actually believe in them,' said Micky. 'You *are* nuts!'

'Who cares,' I said.

I *did* care. I knew I was going to be a laughing stock. But I

felt I owed it to Bindweed. I bent down, pretending to pull up my sock, but I gave her a very fond little pat. I hoped she was pleased. And I knew Mum would be too.

She seemed happy already when she collected us from the After School Club.

'Hello, chickies,' she said, beaming at us.

'You seem in ever such a good mood, Mum. I take it Mr Henry isn't going to get rid of you,' I said.

'The exact opposite!' said Mum. 'I went into his office all of a tremble, and he was actually lovely! He said he was impressed with the way I worked and that I was very good with the customers.'

'Mr Henry said that? But I thought he was always so fierce and horrid!'

'Well, not exactly fierce. Or horrid. But he's always been so serious, keeping watch on all us girls,' said Mum. (It was weird the way the supermarket ladies all called themselves girls, even the ones old enough to be grannies.) 'I thought he was weighing me up, about to give me the chop. Shows what a muddle I can get into! He's actually going to up my wages.'

'Well, it's lovely that he's so pleased with you, Mum. Isn't it, Robin?'

'Clever Mum! So are we having a special treat supper?' Robin asked hopefully, eyeing up Mum's shopping bag. 'Is that ice cream?'

'It certainly is ice cream! And we're going to have chicken too, with new potatoes and salad,' said Mum. 'I used my shop discount card to buy lots of lovely things today.'

'Yay!' said Robin. He chanted all the way home: 'Chicken for supper, yum yum yum, and ice cream too, I hope it's strawberry, but I wish it was chips instead of new potatoes and never mind the boring old salad!' The second he got home he charged off to get Fido out of his cardboard-box kennel, promising to share this feast with him.

I wondered what Bindweed would think of a mini version of this meal. I wasn't sure about the chicken. She hadn't been keen on the fish finger. I thought fairies were probably vegetarian, but maybe she'd like a little chopped-up salad? And everyone liked ice cream, didn't they?

I went into my bedroom, sat down, and fished Bindweed out of my sock. She looked a little rumpled, her cap askew and her curls all over the place.

'At last! I thought you were keeping me tucked down in your sock for ever!' she said, stretching. 'What a long long long

day! I'm so glad fairies don't have to go to school. And why on earth does your mother come to collect you, a great girl like you?'

'She'd worry about Robin and me crossing the road. You know what mums are like,' I said, laying Bindweed gently on my pillow.

She stretched into a starfish shape, and then wriggled over onto her tummy and flapped her wings. They were bent out of shape and took a while to unfold properly.

'I don't know what human mothers are like,' said Bindweed. 'When *our* mothers give birth there's a huge celebration for each little newborn fairy bud. Baby fairies toddle about for a few months generally creating havoc, but as soon as they can fly they look after themselves. I was particularly advanced, entirely independent when I was three months old and no bigger than a ladybird. That is an interesting fairy fact. I would start taking notes for your project right this minute.'

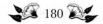

'Oh, I hoped you'd help me!' I said. I reached for my school bag and opened it. 'Oh dear, it's still a bit yucky inside. I don't suppose you can magic it clean again?'

'Fairies aren't washerwomen!' said Bindweed testily. 'We don't stoop to that kind of magic. It's a total waste of our powers. In any case, I doubt I have much left. My enforced hibernation has weakened me considerably. I am fading away.' She held out her little hands to the light. I was alarmed to see that they were semi-transparent. She sighed dramatically and shook them. 'I wouldn't be at all surprised if my poor hands fell right off my arms!'

'Your hands are still strong enough to tie shoelaces,' I said quickly. 'Oh, Bindweed, it was so naughty of you to play that trick on her, though I'm so glad you did it. Poor Cathy looked so funny.'

'*Poor* Cathy? Have a little spirit, please! She's a total monster. You can sit meekly and let her insult you, but I'm not having anyone get the better of my girl,' said Bindweed.

'I'm *your girl*?' I whispered. 'I feel honoured!'

'And so you should be,' said Bindweed. 'Of course, the arrangement is only temporary. Tomorrow you will find me a new home, seeing as my poor dear Wentworth is a bleak ruin

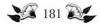

without so much as a blade of grass. What's happened to Ivy and Nettle and Dandelion? Are we all done for now?' Bindweed put her hand to her forehead dramatically. 'Am I the last fairy on earth? Are there only tintack replicas left, like the abominations in your home?'

'Hey, that's ever so rude! Mum's ornaments are very pretty,' I said. *Much prettier than you!* I thought, but I didn't want to hurt her feelings.

Bindweed sniffed dismissively. 'I suppose she doesn't know any better,' she said.

'That's still insulting my mum. If your little bootie things had laces then I might decide to tangle them up when you go to sleep,' I said. 'Then you'd be the one falling flat on your face.' I waited a little anxiously, hoping that she would realize I was only joking.

She raised her tiny eyebrows and sucked in her weeny lips. 'Very funny,' she said, with gritted teeth. 'Do not mock me when I am in the depths of despair.'

'Look, I promise I'll do my very best to find you a new home,' I said. 'It's Saturday tomorrow. I won't have to bunk off school. I'm sure we'll be able to find *somewhere* that suits you. A place with lots of flowers. I know! What about an actual flower shop?'

There was one in the shopping centre. Mum often stood peering in the window at the elaborate floral displays. She liked to watch the customers too. She sighed in sympathy if someone tear-stained trudged in to discuss a funeral wreath. She smiled when young women went in with their mothers to choose a bridal bouquet. She cooed with delight when a man darted in the shop and came out carrying a big bunch of roses for his sweetheart. Valentine's Day was her favourite time of the year, though she never received a single red rose herself.

'A flower *shop*?' Bindweed said doubtfully. 'I don't think that would be at all suitable. Much too confined and with very little scope. I need somewhere outdoors, somewhere green where I can let myself run wild.'

'A big garden?' I suggested. There weren't any proper gardens in our street. And even the parks were just grass and play equipment, no real wild bits. I didn't know anyone with a real garden either. Then I suddenly remembered Mrs Horsley and her beautiful roses!

'My teacher must have a lovely garden,' I said excitedly. 'I could find out where she lives. I know she grows roses there. You said you like roses!'

'I like to *choke* them,' said Bindweed. 'Is your teacher a keen gardener?'

'I think she must be,' I said, wondering how you could choke a plant.

'She keeps her classroom neat and tidy,' said Bindweed. 'I expect she's a keen weeder. I doubt any bindweed would flourish there. Gardeners are my deadly enemy. Would *you* like to be yanked up by your roots and thrown on a dung heap? I speak from personal experience,' she said, clutching her chest at the memory. 'Think again!'

'I'm trying to!' I said, but it was very difficult. 'Look, have a peer in my fairy book to see if you can spot anywhere that seems like your ideal home. And I'll wash out my school bag while Mum's busy in the kitchen.'

I set the book on my bed and opened it for her, hoping she'd be able to manage turning the pages herself, even though they were big as sheets for her. She didn't say thank you. Here was one more fact for my special project: fairies weren't very polite.

I locked myself in the bathroom, ran some water into the sink, and started taking out the slimy contents of my school bag. I wiped my pen and pencils with loo paper and then used soapy

water and a flannel, and dried them with a towel. I was scrupulous about using my own flannel and towel because it only seemed fair. Two of my school textbooks had laminated covers and were quite easy to clean, but my brand-new project book was a nightmare. I managed to clean it, and it didn't smell any more, but the pages were all crinkled and soggy. I'd have to tell Mrs Horsley it fell in the bath. I was worrying about the many lies I was telling, but if I told her truthfully that a fairy had been sick in my school bag she'd think I'd gone bananas.

Then I had a good scrub in the bag, using a lot of bubble bath to make it smell really fresh, and it came up as good as new. Well, almost. I wiped it dry carefully and came out of the bathroom with a light heart. Then I bumped into Mum.

'I was just about to knock! Supper's ready, sweetheart. Are you all right? You've been ages in there,' she said. She peered at my school bag. 'You weren't doing your homework on the toilet, were you?' she asked.

'I – I needed to sort something out,' I said.

'You're a funny little sausage,' Mum said. She put her arm round me and steered me into the kitchen. Bindweed would simply have to wait. She had lots of pictures to look at after all.

Supper was lovely: cold chicken, tomatoes, cucumber,

lettuce, sweetcorn and little new potatoes dabbed with butter.

'It seems very extravagant, even counting in my new pay rise, but I thought it was a day of celebration,' said Mum.

'And there's ice cream for pudding?' Robin checked.

'Yes there is, darling. Strawberry!' said Mum.

Robin smacked his lips appreciatively. I sidled to the kitchen drawer and pretended I was searching for the box of tissues. I was actually looking for our matchbox. Luckily, there weren't too many matches in it. I emptied them out as silently as I could and slipped the box into my hand. I didn't want to gum up my pocket again, and salad and ice cream all slopped together wouldn't be appetizing, no matter how delicious individually.

Mum and Robin both talked non-stop throughout the meal, Mum repeating Mr Henry's compliments, and Robin yacking away about playing mummies and daddies with his little girlfriends in the playground.

'I was the daddy, of course, and I promised my wife and daughters I would never ever leave them,' Robin said.

Mum choked on her chicken and looked as if she might cry. 'Of course you wouldn't, darling,' she said.

Luckily, she was so pleased about Mr Henry giving her a wage rise that she didn't get *too* upset. She started talking about

his plans for a bigger salad bar in the supermarket, with a much wider variety of choices.

'Mr Henry says more people are into healthy eating now. And we're going to introduce more vegan options too. He's got such good ideas,' said Mum.

I nodded and smiled at her, while stealthily transferring a sliver of tomato and cucumber, a couple of golden corn seeds and the tiniest leaf off the heart of the lettuce to the matchbox. I didn't add a piece of potato because Bindweed didn't seem to care for hot food. Then I concentrated on my own meal and ate it all up. I risked transferring a big spoonful of ice cream to the matchbox too, praying it wouldn't thaw too rapidly.

'That was the yummiest meal ever!' said Robin. 'Even the salad was nice, apart from the green bits. I don't really see the point of cucumber and lettuce.'

Bindweed liked her cucumber and lettuce most of all. She spurned the tomato and sweetcorn.

'I don't recognize these fruits,' she said. 'But generally bright colours are to be avoided. Many are deadly poisonous. I haven't survived being squashed in a book for many many years simply to succumb to death by bellyache.'

She liked the ice cream most of all, though she had to scoop it up in her fingers. 'Wild strawberries are my favourite snack! How clever to mix them up with this cold cream! I feel *so* much better!' she said, smacking her little lips.

Her wings fluttered joyfully, the green veins darker, forming a beautiful pattern. Her long hair grew curlier and shone with new emerald vigour.

'I'm so glad we've found something you really like,' I said. 'I'll ask Mum if we can have lots of salad. She'll be pleased, because it's very good for us. I don't think she'll let us have ice cream every day, but I can always ask.'

'But I won't be here, will I? You're going to find me a new home,' said Bindweed.

'I know. I promised. It's the topmost problem in my mind,' I said. 'Still, while we're still looking for the right place, could you possibly help me with my fairy project? *You* promised.'

'Very well. We must get to work,' said Bindweed. She bounced across my bed to the open book of fairy paintings. 'Most of these paintings are *totally* erroneous!'

'What does that mean?' I asked.

Bindweed sighed heavily. 'You're so ignorant, Miss Mab! It means they are inaccurate. Ludicrously so! Figments of someone's warped imagination. These painters have never seen a fairy in their lives.'

'So I can't write about them for my fairy project?' I said, disappointed. 'Each painting has a lot of writing beside it, so I thought I could copy a lot of it to make my project look impressive. I wanted to try to copy some of the paintings too.'

'Write about them if you must, but why waste your time copying the artwork when they are so gross?' said Bindweed, poking one of the paintings of a flying fairy with a disdainful finger.

'She's not gross!' I argued. I read the title of the painting: *Iris*. 'You should like her. She's a flower fairy like you. She's called Iris.'

'No decent fairy would fly around stark naked!' said Bindweed primly. 'She's very vulgar!'

'Naked figures aren't rude if they're in a painting,' I said – though I knew Mum thought them very rude even so, and they made Robin shriek with laughter.

'I happen to have made the acquaintance of many wild iris fairies in my time, and though they were flighty girls, they were always decently dressed in purple or yellow frocks, with caps and slippers to match. And their wings were rather splendid – powerful and strongly veined, not these pathetic glittery protuberances,' said Bindweed.

I wasn't sure what that meant either, but as she'd got so tetchy before I didn't like to ask.

'How could she possibly fly with those stunted little wings?' she declared. 'And in that bizarre position too, arms folded, legs together! As if that would ever work! I think that artist simply wanted to paint somebody naked.'

'What about these fairies then?' I said, turning the pages. 'They've all got big wings and long dresses. I think they're quite pretty.'

Bindweed sniffed. 'Then you have no taste,' she said.

'And you have no manners!' I retorted.

To my surprise she chuckled. 'That's the spirit,' she said. 'You must learn to stand up for yourself. I am amazed you let those tedious girls in your class make fun of you.'

'They call me names,' I said.

'Then call them names too, worse ones. And play tricks on them. That is the fairy way,' said Bindweed.

'I think the fairy way might get me into trouble,' I said. 'Actually, I'm *already* in trouble. Cathy's mum thinks I knocked her over on purpose and hurt her leg.'

'Serves her right,' said Bindweed.

'Yes, but suppose she'd really been hurt?' I said.

'You're so *kind*!' said Bindweed. She said it as if it was an insult. 'You wouldn't last five minutes if you were me. We bindweeds are tough and fierce and determined. We cling and choke to survive. That's why we've lasted through the centuries. We may appear fragile, but we have spirits of steel, come what may. I daresay *you* wouldn't have survived being squashed in a book for years!'

'I don't suppose I would,' I agreed humbly.

'That is what I wish you to emphasize in your project,' said Bindweed. 'The superior character of the convolvulus family! It's strongly disputed, of course, but the bindweeds and their

lesser cousins are actually the kings and queens of all the flower fairies, indeed the entire fairy world. Take your notebook and write that down for your project.'

I discovered that the pages of my notebook were too puckered and wrinkly to write on, so I had to use my big drawing book instead. It had large blank pages and I've got small, squashed-up handwriting, but I'd filled one whole page by the time Mum called me into the living room.

'What have you been up to, Mab? It's nearly bedtime!' she said, patting the sofa so I could come and snuggle up beside her. Robin was on her lap, sucking his thumb while she read him a story.

'I've been working hard on my school project,' I said, for once telling the absolute truth.

'What's the subject then?' Mum asked.

I took a deep breath. 'Fairies!' I said.

'Oh, Mab! Seriously? Oh, darling, that's fantastic!' said Mum, her eyes shining. All the eyes of the china and pewter and plaster fairies seemed to gleam too, and the fairy lights flashed. 'Perhaps I could help you?' Mum added eagerly. 'I've learned quite a bit about fairy folk.'

'Well, thanks, Mum – but I'd really like to do all the

research myself,' I said. I knew Mum's take on fairies was never going to chime with Bindweed's.

'Don't worry, I understand. We don't want Mrs Horsley to think you've been cheating,' said Mum. 'Hey, I wonder if you'll be allowed to present your project wearing your fairy dress?'

'Yes, I wonder,' I said carefully.

'Anyway, cuddle up. I'm reading *Peter Pan* to Robin,' said Mum.

'Peter tells you to clap hands if you believe in fairies to save Tinkerbell's life,' said Robin. 'I clapped, didn't I, Mum?' He paused. 'Even though I'm not sure I really *do* believe in fairies now I'm older.'

'Robin!' said Mum. 'Five's not *old*. I believe in fairies and I'm not *old* old!'

'Some of my friends at school say fairies are silly,' said Robin.

'I bet they don't say that about the tooth fairy,' I teased.

'Well, you don't believe in fairies, do you?' Robin persisted.

'I do, actually,' I said.

'Um, that's a fib,' said Robin.

'No it's not. It's the absolute truth,' I declared.

'Oh, Mab,' said Mum. She looked incredibly touched.

'You don't have to believe just to please me. I know a lot of people think I'm completely bonkers. I told one of the girls at work that I'd bought you a fairy frock for your birthday and she pulled this face and said, "I thought your daughter was in the Juniors? Isn't she a bit old for that lark?"'

'Well, I'm not,' I said. 'I love my fairy dress. It's my best birthday present ever.' That *wasn't* the absolute truth. In fact, it was a downright lie, but it couldn't be helped. 'Mum, I know Peter Pan and Tinkerbell lived in Neverland, which is a made-up place, but where did he live before that?'

'In Kensington Gardens,' said Mum. 'And that's definitely real because I used to go past it on the bus every day when I worked in this big hotel.'

'And are Kensington Gardens *actual* gardens?' I asked. 'All garden and no big blocks of flats?'

'Yes, huge gardens. And I think they've got a statue of Peter Pan there. I've seen a picture of it in one of my fairy mags.'

'Could we go and see the statue then? And the rest of the gardens? Do you think they're the sort of gardens where fairies might like to live now?'

'Well, *I* would,' said Mum.

'Could we maybe go there tomorrow, on the bus, to have a

look? Then I could write about it for my project?' I asked.

'Well, it's a really long bus ride away from here but I suppose so. All right then, darling, we'll have a lovely Saturday out,' said Mum.

I gave her a hug. Maybe I'd found a new home for Bindweed, just as I'd promised!

CHAPTER ELEVEN

'Have you heard of a place called Kensington Gardens?' I asked Bindweed as I tucked her up in my slipper under the bed.

'I don't think so,' she said.

'Well, we're going there tomorrow. It's Saturday so I don't have to wear school uniform. I'm going to wear a dress with a proper pocket. I'll pop you in it and it'll be much more comfortable than my school bag or my sock. Mum says these gardens are huge, and fairies used to live there, so I think I've found you a new home just like I promised,' I said proudly.

'Really?' said Bindweed, bouncing out of my slipper and turning a cartwheel. She looked so sweet and tiny and happy that I felt a sudden pang. She'd become part of my life now. Even though she could be very demanding at times, I realized I was going to miss her tremendously.

'Unless you decide that you wanted to stay here,' I said casually.

Bindweed blinked at me.

'But there's no greenery,' she said.

'Well, they sell plants down the market. Maybe I could get Mum to buy some.' I didn't know much about them. The only thing I'd ever grown was some mustard and cress on an old flannel, but I didn't think Bindweed would count that as greenery. We had a strange plant called a spider plant on the windowsill in Mrs Horsley's class. It was quite interesting because it grew little baby spider plants at the ends of its fronds.

'How about a spider plant?' I suggested.

'A *spider* plant,' said Bindweed doubtfully. 'Not *real* spiders I hope! How big are they? Could you possibly fill your small dwelling with them?'

'I think we'd have to stick to one spider plant,' I said. 'But they're quite big compared to you.' I gestured with my hands.

Bindweed rolled her green eyes. 'I could choke that in half an hour,' she said.

'You're meant to feed and water plants and give them lots of daylight,' I said. 'Why do you always want to *choke* them?'

'It's my nature,' said Bindweed. '*I* feed and drink from them and steal their daylight. We bindweeds are world experts. They employed a whole team of doltish gardeners at Wentworth, who battled hard to beat us, but we rioted all over the grounds and sprang out triumphantly from every hedge. We were the bane of their lives.'

I sighed. Even with Mum's rise in salary I knew we could never provide enough plants for bindweed to riot in. I couldn't help thrilling at the idea of turning our flat into a garden centre so that bindweeds could trail over the bed, climb the curtains, and criss-cross the ceiling, but I knew it wouldn't be allowed. Even though Mum was completely better, we still had visits from a social worker every now and then to check up on us.

We used to have a kind cheerful lady called Arit who gave us cuddles, even Mum, but now we had Mrs Wright, who was old and bossy and a real know-it-all. She was always fussing about health and safety, and worried about Mum's fairy lights and the state of Fido, whose coat might once have been cream

coloured but was now a strange shade of sludge. Goodness knows what she'd say if she found our flat taken over by a jungle.

'I suppose it wouldn't work,' I said sadly. 'Oh well, let's hope Kensington Gardens is a lovely place. Though I will miss you tremendously if you stay there, Bindweed.'

She looked up at me curiously. 'I don't think I've ever been missed before,' she said. 'People generally detest me and my kin. I am called the gardener's curse, a creeping killer. Folk like to take fistfuls of my fronds, pull them up by the roots and then burn them in bonfires. I've lost count of the massacres I've witnessed.'

I reached down and scooped her up. 'Why don't you come and lie on my pillow for a bit? I'm sure it's a bit stuffy in my slipper. Mum's just washed the sheets so they smell lovely, like lilac.'

'Really?' said Bindweed. She wriggled out of my grasp and buried her head in the pillow. 'Mm! That's not like any lilac I've ever smelled – but I suppose it's reasonably pleasant,' she admitted.

She seemed to be trying to be reasonably pleasant herself. Neither of us were at all sleepy, so we lay on our backs and chatted. Bindweed tested me on my fairy knowledge. She gave

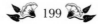

me a poke if I got anything wrong, but a little pat with her tiny hand if I answered correctly. I couldn't help feeling her fairy history was a little biased, because the bindweeds and their lesser cousins were always the most brave, handsome, courageous, successful fairies, superior in every way.

'And can fairies really grant wishes?' I asked her.

'It depends,' said Bindweed. 'If they feel so inclined, I daresay fairies can do anything. Not common little buds like the daisies or the buttercups, or even those snooty wild orchids who think themselves so precious, but bindweeds quite definitely have the power.'

'So . . . could you grant *me* a wish?' I asked.

Bindweed looked at me, considering. 'I'm still weak from my long hibernation, but I think I could summon up the energy to grant something simple. Would you like me to play another trick on that Cathy person? I could curdle her milk in a trice.'

'Curdle her milk?' I repeated, baffled.

'When she's milked the family cow and put the bowl in the dairy,' said Bindweed.

'Cathy hasn't got a *cow*!' I said. 'You don't keep farm animals at home nowadays. Some people keep chickens, but only if they've got gardens. The housing association won't let

us have any pets at all in our flat. Well, the lady upstairs has a budgie, but she keeps it in a cage.'

'Doesn't your little brother have the Fido creature?' Bindweed asked.

'Yes, but he's not a *real* dog,' I said. 'I don't suppose you could turn him into a real dog, could you, Bindweed?' I asked, side-tracked. Maybe it was time *I* started breaking a few rules too!

'I hardly think that would be wise. Fido would take one look at me and gobble me up in a trice,' said Bindweed. 'Focus on Cathy. I daresay I could conjure up a few warts on her nose.'

I couldn't help a wicked giggle at the thought of Cathy's pretty little snub nose with warts all over it. But it seemed such a mean thing to do. And suppose they were permanent?

'I really don't want you to do that, Bindweed,' I said.

My virtue didn't impress her one bit. 'You are such a sap,' she said. 'No fun at all. A pathetic little mouse of a girl. Ah!'

'What do you mean, "ah"?' I asked warily.

'How about I inflict a plague of mice on her dwelling place? Or perhaps I could go the whole hog and make them rats?' said Bindweed.

'Stop it! That's awful!' I said, although I had a sudden

image of Cathy and her horrid mum rushing around screaming their heads off with mice running up and down their legs.
'Promise me you won't ever do anything like that,' I added,
a little reluctantly.

'There's no need to fuss so. I was only teasing. I'm not at all
keen on rodents myself. Some of my fellow fairies tame them
and ride them when they need to give their wings a rest, but
I've never cared for the idea. Those teeth could inflict a nasty
bite,' said Bindweed.

'Don't you ever grant lovely wishes?' I asked.

'I've never felt the urge,' said Bindweed. She stretched her
small limbs and then wriggled a little nearer until she was
curled up in the palm of my hand. 'But I suppose I could try.
Tell me your heart's desire.'

'Well . . . I want my dad to come back. Not really for me
– I'm still angry at him for walking out on us. It's for Mum. It
would make her really happy again.'

'I said *your* heart. I don't want to strain myself granting
wishes for all your family.'

I thought really hard.

'I suppose what I'd really really like . . .' I began.

'Yes? Spit it out!' said Bindweed.

'I'd like Billie to be friends with me again. Not just a little bit friendly behind Cathy's back. Proper friends, like we were before,' I said wistfully.

Bindweed gave me a look. 'I'm not sure it's worth summoning up all my magical powers on such a paltry wish,' she said.

'What does *paltry* mean?' I asked. 'I wish you wouldn't use such difficult words all the time. Oh, that wasn't my *wish* wish!'

'Just as well. I don't see why I should use baby talk when I'm a mature fairy of a hundred and eighty or so,' said Bindweed. 'Try a proper wish. Challenge me!'

I tried hard to think of something. I didn't want to mess up this one chance.

'Can I have a little think about my wish and ask you tomorrow?'

'Very well,' said Bindweed. She yawned and wriggled. 'It's been a long day. I'm rather tired now. I wonder if you could return me to your slipper. It's very comfortable up here, but I don't want to get squashed all over again if you lie on me. Don't take offence, but you are rather a great lump of a girl.'

'No I'm not! And you mustn't call anyone "a great lump" – that's fat-shaming,' I said indignantly.

'I can call anyone anything I like,' said Bindweed. 'Fairies and their kin positively delight in name-calling. My goodness, you should have heard the boggarts who lived in a ditch at Wentworth!'

'What's a boggart? They don't sound very nice,' I said.

'Boggarts are crude, hairy creatures who live in dark, slimy places and make mischief – though they're generally harmless.' Bindweed yawned again. 'Bedtime!'

'Please couldn't you tell me more about fairy creatures?' I asked. 'Do boggarts have hair all over, like monkeys? What exactly is a pixie? Is it the same as a fairy? And what about goblins?'

'Oh, for goodness' sake! Haven't I told you enough about fairies? Do I really have to talk my way through the entire world of magical creatures, good and bad?' Bindweed complained.

'Just a few? Oh, Bindweed, it's probably our last night together. Please talk to me just a little bit more,' I begged.

'I'm tired!' Bindweed whined.

'Just for ten minutes?'

She sighed so deeply that she made a little breeze. 'Very well. Though it would take ten thousand minutes to describe every species of the fairy kingdom,' she said.

'Can I take notes for my fairy project?' I asked, jumping out of bed and grabbing my drawing book.

She dictated wearily while I scribbled, though her voice kept fading as she fell asleep. I stroked her gently each time, and she sighed and continued, doing her best. Then she started snoring. It was the funniest little sound, like a cat purring, and I didn't have the heart to wake her up yet again. I wanted her to stay on the pillow beside me so I could look at her in the moonlight. I was sure I wouldn't roll on her and squash her.

I lay down very carefully, trying not to disturb her, but she opened one green eye.

'Slipper!' she murmured.

So I scooped her up carefully, hung over the bed and inserted her into the slipper. I gave her long green curls a very gentle stroke, and then settled down to sleep myself.

I dreamed about pixies and goblins and boggarts, and when I woke up in the morning I wondered just for an instance if Bindweed herself was part of the dream – but when I peered under the bed she was lying there in my slipper, her cap awry, and her thumb in her mouth. She might be a hundred and eighty, but she looked like a little fairy baby when she was fast asleep.

Robin was wide awake. I could hear him skipping around the flat, singing, 'We're going to see Peter Pan today, hippy hippy hip hip hooray!'

'You sound happy,' I said, going into the bathroom.

'Yes I am, because *we're going to see Peter Pan today, hippy hippy hip hip hooray*! Did you hear it, Mab?' Robin called through the door. 'It's my song and I made it up all by myself.'

'I heard it, and it's very clever,' I said.

'Did you hear all the words? They rhyme! *We're going to see*

Peter Pan today, hippy hippy hip hip hooray! Did you get it? Shall I sing it again?' Robin persisted.

He sang it again whether I wanted to hear it or not. He sang it again and again, until he nearly drove Mum and me mad, but it was sweet that he was so excited.

Mum agreed that we could go straight after breakfast, once we were washed and dressed.

'Are you going to wear your fairy frock, Mab?' Robin asked.

Mum looked up eagerly. 'You can if you really want to,' she said.

I so *didn't* want to. I sought wildly for an excuse. 'It might get all dirty and muddy in the gardens,' I said.

'You're not going to roll in the grass, are you?' said Mum, giving me a sideways look.

'Of course not, but – but it's not very warm today and I think I need to wear a cardie, which would look silly with my fairy dress. Besides, the wings might get crumpled,' I said.

I wore my check dress with the handy pocket and my blue cardigan on top. Bindweed was safely hidden, but able to peep out occasionally whenever she fancied. Robin continued to sing his Peter Pan song at the top of his voice, though Mum tried her best to stop him, especially when we walked past the

parade of shops with her supermarket at the end.

People's heads kept turning, and a tall, good-looking man standing at the entrance of Mum's supermarket smiled at him.

'Hey, young man, that's a splendid song!' he said.

'Hello, Mr Henry!' said Mum, all of a flutter.

Mr Henry? He wasn't remotely like a squat little vacuum cleaner!

'Robin, stop that singing at once!' said Mum, giving his arm a little shake. 'Say hello to Mr Henry, my boss. And this is my daughter, Mab.'

'Hello!' said Robin cheerfully, not at all subdued.

'Hello,' I mumbled, utterly confused.

'So I guess you're all going to see Peter Pan,' said Mr Henry. 'I thought that was a Christmas show.'

'It's just the Peter Pan statue in Kensington Gardens,' Mum said, blushing.

'Oh, that's a great idea,' said Mr Henry. 'My mum used to take us kids there when we were little. There's this round pond where posh little kids sail their boats. I tried to sail a huge chunk of wood instead, and it torpedoed one of the biggest boats and sank it, and Mum didn't half give me what for!'

'What's a what-for?' Robin asked.

'A cuff about the head,' said Mr Henry, grinning. 'And I probably deserved it.'

'My mum would never give me a cuff,' said Robin, shocked.

'Of course she wouldn't. She's obviously a lovely mum,' said Mr Henry.

Mum was rosy pink by now. 'Well, we'd better get going

then,' she said. She nodded shyly. 'Nice to see you, Mr Henry.'

'Nice to see you too, Mrs Macclesfield,' he said solemnly, but it sounded as if he was teasing her.

'Who's that man, Mum?' Robin asked as we walked on.

'Ssh! He's my boss,' said Mum.

'But I thought he was all mean and strict. That man was funny and smiley,' said Robin, without remotely lowering his voice.

'Will you *shush*!' Mum hissed. 'I *did* think he was a bit strict at first, but he was only getting things sorted out. He's very kind.'

Robin lost interest and started singing his Peter Pan song again. And again.

'You don't think he thought I was walking past on purpose, do you?' Mum asked me, suddenly looking appalled.

'Of course not. You have to go past the shop to get to the bus stop,' I said.

'I know. But perhaps *he* doesn't know. I wish we'd gone round the long way now,' said Mum. She sighed. 'What did you think of him anyway?'

'I don't know. He's OK,' I said. I peered at her. 'What are you getting in such a state about, Mum?'

'Well, I need to stay on his good side,' said Mum. 'And I feel bad. The shop looked crowded already. He might wonder what I was doing, swanning off to Kensington Gardens instead of working.'

'But you've never worked at the weekends, Mum. That's our time,' I said.

'Yes, but I've never been given a raise before,' said Mum.

'Oh, Mum, I wish you'd stop worrying about everything,' I said.

Bindweed craned upwards in my pocket until I could see the tiny stalk of her green cap. Perhaps she thought it was a real wish. It would be a waste. I didn't think all the fairies in the world could stop Mum worrying.

I tried to remember what she'd been like when Dad was with us and we were a proper family. She'd seemed just as anxious then, probably because Dad stayed out a lot playing his music and seemed in a dream half the time when he was at home. He didn't shout and he didn't sulk, he simply drifted about as if he wasn't really there. Or he sat and watched old movies – he especially loved the old Jurassic Park films.

I hated thinking about the things that happened next, after Dad went out one evening to play a gig and didn't come back.

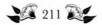

Ever. So I joined in Robin's Peter Pan song to distract myself. Luckily we were the only people waiting at the bus stop, but when we got on the bus Mum begged us both to stop.

'Let's sit at the top of the bus and pretend we're driving it,' I suggested to Robin. I was too old to play at bus drivers but I knew it would be a good way to stop him singing.

Mum smiled at me gratefully. 'You'll be such a good mum one day, Mab,' she said.

I wasn't sure I ever wanted to be a mum – or have a partner. I wanted to live in a little attic room all by myself and paint all day, maybe with a cat for company. It might be a bit lonely sometimes, but it would be peaceful.

Bindweed was starting to fidget now, tickling my tummy as she moved about restlessly.

I bent down, pretending to adjust the laces on my shoe. 'What's the matter?' I whispered.

'This monstrous vehicle is jerking us around in a most unpleasant way. I'm starting to feel so sick!'

'Oh, please don't be sick in my pocket!' I whispered.

'Thank you for being so sympathetic!' Bindweed snapped sarcastically. 'Oh, my stomach! My ears!'

'Your *ears*?' I said. How could her ears feel sick?

'The noise!' Bindweed explained. 'The terrible roaring noise!'

I presumed she meant the sound of the bus, but there was nothing I could do to make it softer. I straightened up, because I was starting to feel sick myself in that position. Robin was staring at me.

'What's the matter with my ears?' he said.

'Nothing! I mean, I like your ears,' I said. 'They look very . . . neat.'

They did actually look quite sweet, showing small and pink under his mop of curls.

Robin rubbed his ears self-consciously. 'You are weird sometimes,' he said, but raised his hands to hold an imaginary steering wheel. '*Brm brm*, out of my way, silly old cars, or I'll bump my bus right into you.' It didn't look as if Robin was going to be a very considerate driver when he grew up. While he was terrorizing traffic I slipped my hand in my pocket and tried to stroke Bindweed, but she pushed me away, groaning softly.

I had a sudden idea. 'Mum, I feel a bit sick,' I said, and lolled my head pathetically.

'Oh dear,' said Mum. 'Have a peppermint – that might make you feel a bit better.' She poked around in her handbag

 213

for her little box of mints and gave me one. She gave one to Robin too, because he never wanted to be left out.

I pretended to put it in my mouth but deftly slipped it into my pocket instead. 'It'll make you feel better!' I said softly. 'Sorry it's so big.'

Robin blinked. His neat ears were also very sharp. 'It's not big. They're about the smallest sweets ever. One crunch and they're gone!'

It would be like sticking an entire loaf of peppermint into a fairy mouth, but I hoped Bindweed would have the sense to take little licks. She was obviously finding it helpful, because she stopped flopping about and moaning after a little while.

I concentrated on the view from the windows, staring at all the big brick buildings. If they seemed huge to me, even sitting at the top of the bus, then they'd be terrifyingly tall to Bindweed. I strained my eyes, but couldn't see any greenery apart from the odd hanging basket or window ledge, and I could see those wouldn't be a very satisfactory fairy home. But at last I saw a gleam of green and then a whole wide expanse as far as I could see.

'We're here!' said Mum, pressing the bell for the bus to stop. 'Hold my hand, Robin. We have to get off now.

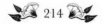

We're at Kensington Gardens!'

They weren't like any garden I'd ever seen. They were absolutely vast, with long stretches of grass and sandy paths as far as the eye could see. I felt stirring inside my pocket. Bindweed was peeping out too, though her hands were over her ears because of the roar of the traffic going past.

'It's very noisy but I think it will get much quieter when we're right inside the gardens,' I announced, so that she could hear.

'Where's Peter Pan then?' said Robin, peering round.

'I'm not quite sure, chickie. We'll just have a wander. I'm sure we'll find him,' said Mum.

We had a very long wander. We came across the round pond that Mr Henry had mentioned. There were children playing with boats, exactly as he'd said, and even some grown-ups with fancy motorized miniature yachts. There were quite a few women with babies in buggies. Mum whispered that they were probably nannies. I stared at them with interest, but none of them looked like Mary Poppins.

Robin was disappointed too. 'I wish one was a nanny dog like Nana in *Peter Pan*,' he said.

Robin pretended to be a dog himself, gambolling about

sniffing the grass, and then running all the way round the pond until he had to throw himself on the grass, breathless.

Mum took out a bottle of water from her handbag and gave him a drink. I had some too. I'd have liked to offer Bindweed a thimbleful, but it was too public and someone might see. I peered all round, looking for a quiet secluded spot behind a hedge, but it was all so open, everything trimmed so neatly, and there were people everywhere. Maybe Kensington Gardens was the wrong place for her to live after all. I couldn't see any bindweed flowers anywhere.

I hoped Peter Pan might be in a better place. It took us a long time to find him, right the other side of the gardens.

'Is *that* Peter Pan?' Robin cried.

It was a terrible disappointment. He was a dark grey statue with a pudding basin haircut and he seemed to be wearing a frock.

'Why is he wearing a dress?' Robin asked.

'It's not a dress, it's a kind of tunic,' said Mum.

'Well, it looks silly,' said Robin.

It did, rather, and Peter Pan himself looked silly too, holding a little horn to his lips and pointing his feet. He had a strange grey girl peering up at him, and odd little creatures all

round his plinth, but none looked like proper fairies. There were real children trying to climb up him too, though they kept being scolded for it. It was noisier than the Infants playground at dinner time.

I could feel Bindweed sinking to the bottom of my pocket in despair. I'd promised to find her a home, and I'd failed miserably.

CHAPTER TWELVE

We were all disappointed, but when we came out of the gardens we saw an ice-cream van. We had cones to cheer ourselves up. I broke off the end of mine and scooped a morsel of ice cream on top, making a miniature cornet. I popped it into my pocket when no one was looking. Bindweed ate her custom-made cone in secret. I had to eat the rest of mine very quickly because the ice cream started dripping out of the cone and dribbling up my arm. I licked it off, not wanting to waste it.

'Mucky pup,' said Mum, but fondly. 'Shall we have a little explore down the road while we're here? I think there are some museums further along.'

'Museums?' Robin and I repeated, without enthusiasm.

'Museums are lovely places,' said Mum. 'Do you know, there's an actual fairy museum in America!'

'A fairy museum!' I said. There was a stirring in my pocket. 'You mean *real* fairies?'

Mum looked at me. 'Well, not real, obviously. But replicas. There's an article about them in my *Fairy* mag. There are all sorts of displays. You keep going down dark tunnels dimly lit with fairy lanterns, and then when you turn a corner there's a glass cabinet all lit up and you see these lovely little fairies dancing around. Some actually fly! It looks so lifelike. They play beautiful tinkly fairy music and all the attendants are dressed as fairies, even the *toilet* attendant. Imagine!

'The cafe has a fairy theme, so you can have elderflower juice and rosehip muffins. You can have an actual birthday party there where you get a big pink-and-white iced birthday cake with a fairy on the top, a different one according to your birth sign. You're Cancer, Mab, so you'd get a fairy with a silver frock and matching wings. I wish I could have got you a silver fairy outfit – I know you're not that keen on pink.'

Robin was yawning. 'Do they have a goblin museum too?' he asked. 'Um, that's a rude word, isn't it? Gob gob gob!'

'Robin!' said Mum, sighing. 'Don't be silly.'

'I like pink,' I fibbed. 'And the fairy museum sounds lovely, Mum.' That was another fib. I thought it sounded incredibly yucky. From the sounds coming from my pocket Bindweed thought so too.

'I'd give anything to have been able to take you there for your birthday, Mab,' said Mum.

'Well, maybe one day I'll take you there for *your* birthday, Mum,' I said. When I'd won the lottery. I was pretty certain Bindweed's wishes weren't the sort that could fly us over the Atlantic to this fairy museum, especially as it would cost hundreds and hundreds of pounds.

'No, *I'll* take you to my goblin museum and we'll all go "*gob gob gob*",' said Robin, demonstrating.

'Robin! Stop that or we'll take you home straight away and shut you in Fido's kennel,' I said sternly, trying to grab him.

Robin dodged away from me and barged into an old man in a posh stripy blazer and panama hat.

'*Robin!*' Mum cried, mortified. 'I'm so sorry, sir. He didn't mean to bump into you. He's just got over-excited. Tell the gentleman you're very sorry, Robin!'

'Sorry!' Robin mumbled.

'That's all right, laddie. You're only young once. I bet you're excited about seeing the dinosaurs, eh?'

'*Dinosaurs?*' Robin repeated. 'You don't get dinosaurs now, only in films.'

Dad had left several old Jurassic Park DVDs behind when he moved out. Mum told us he'd loved dinosaurs and had had a whole collection of plastic dinosaurs when he was a little boy. 'I remember them!' Robin had said, though of course he couldn't remember Dad as a little boy. He couldn't even properly remember Dad when he was our dad, because Robin had been so little when he left.

He still insisted he loved Dad's dinosaur movies, though he only watched through his fingers and often had nightmares afterwards.

'You ask your mother if you can pop into the Natural History Museum, my boy. You'll see lots of dinosaurs inside. You can hear them roar and see them moving about!' said the man in the blazer. He winked at Mum. She didn't wink back. She looked horrified. The man tipped his hat to her and then sauntered off, not realizing he'd caused a big problem.

'I want to go to the dinosaur museum!' said Robin.

'I think it's a bit too old for you, darling,' said Mum.

'No it's not! That man in the funny stripy jacket *said* I should go,' Robin pleaded.

'Then he should have minded his own business,' said Mum. 'I know you wouldn't like it.'

'I know I would!' said Robin. 'And Mab would like it too, wouldn't you, Mab?'

I did rather want to go. Billie had been taken to see the dinosaurs at the museum and said they were wicked. But I knew Mum was right not to let Robin go.

'They'll be too scary for you,' I said.

'No they won't! I'm not ever ever scared of dinosaurs. I love them. My *dad* liked them,' said Robin, nodding his head insistently.

'Oh, Robin,' said Mum, and for a terrifying moment I thought she was going to burst into tears. She swallowed hard. She so wanted to keep Robin loving Dad even though it was obvious he was never ever coming back. I wished he hadn't sent that birthday card to me. It had stirred her up all over again. 'All right then. We'll go and see the dinosaurs. And maybe we'll go and see if we can find a little toy dinosaur just like Dad had when he was your age,' she said.

I sighed. Mum misunderstood.

'And we'll get you a dinosaur too, Mab,' she said.

'I don't want a stupid dinosaur,' I said crossly. Then I felt bad. I always feel so worried when I'm rude to Mum because she's so easily upset. 'Anyway, I bet it'll be very expensive to get into this museum. We won't be able to afford it,' I added.

But it turned out you didn't have to pay anything to get into the museum, not even to go and see the dinosaurs. We went to the gift shop first, and Mum let Robin rootle amongst all the little triceratops and iguanodons and multiple Tyrannosaurus rex. He wanted one of the T-rexes and couldn't choose for ages, though they all looked identical.

'How about this one? It's got a smiley face,' Mum suggested.

'I don't want a smiley one. I want a fierce one,' said Robin.

I pulled my own fierce face and wandered off to look at all the other toys. They had some amazing furry tarantulas that looked incredibly lifelike. I thought of Micky and his spider project.

'Mum, can I have a tarantula please, if it's not too much money?' I asked.

'That great big hairy spider?' Mum shook her head at both of us. 'I've got two very weird children!' But she bought the

spider and made Robin close his eyes and do a lucky dip into the tray of Tyrannosaurus rexes.

'Yes, this is the best of all of them!' said Robin, kissing its little reptile head. 'I'm going to call him Tyrone. What are you going to call your spider, Mab?'

'It's not a pet – it's going to be part of a spider project for school,' I said loftily.

Mum looked disappointed. 'I thought you were doing a fairy project,' she said.

'I am. Micky Flynn's doing a spider project. I thought he could pass the spider round the class so we could all see what a tarantula looks like,' I said.

'Ha! Micky Flynn's your boyfriend!' said Robin.

'No he's not – he's a mate,' I said.

'Isn't Micky the naughty boy who's always in trouble?' Mum asked.

I sighed. Mum always said this about Micky. 'He's not really naughty. He only messes about a bit. He can be really kind sometimes,' I said.

'See, Mab loves him!' Robin grinned.

'I do *not*!' I said. 'I'll poison you with my tarantula if you don't stop it!'

'Well, my dinosaur will bite its head off and go gollop gollop gollop,' said Robin, waving Tyrone at me.

'Will you please simmer down, both of you,' said Mum. 'Put that horrible spider in your pocket, Mab – it's giving me the creeps.'

I couldn't put it in my pocket because I was certain it would give Bindweed the creeps too.

'Couldn't you put it in your bag, Mum?' I asked.

'If I must,' said Mum, taking hold of it gingerly. 'Do you want to pop your dinosaur in my bag too, Robin?'

'No. Tyrone wants to roam free and frighten people,' said Robin.

'You'd better keep him well under control!' Mum warned. 'Let's go and show him the real dinosaurs then.'

Robin stopped. 'They're not *really* real, are they, Mum?'

'No, they're just very lifelike models, that's all,' said Mum. 'They've got a special exhibition. But we don't have to go and see them if you don't want to.'

'I do want to, ever so! Then when my daddy comes back I can tell him all about them,' said Robin.

'Oh, darling,' said Mum, and she looked as if she might cry again. 'That's a good idea.'

 225

It was a hopelessly bad idea, because Dad was never ever coming back. It was silly of Mum to encourage Robin to think like that. He was only little and didn't understand. When dads cleared off without even bothering to say goodbye, it surely meant they stayed away for ever.

I always made out I didn't care, but it felt like someone was punching me hard in the stomach just thinking it. I actually started to double up with the pain of it, but remembered Bindweed in my pocket and stopped, because I didn't want to squash her.

'Mab? What's the matter, love?' Mum asked.

'It's just . . . just a little squeezy pain in my tummy,' I mumbled.

'Do you need to go to the loo?'

I didn't, but I nodded. We found the ladies' room, and I locked myself in a cubicle, sat on the toilet, spread my dress out and wept silently. After a few seconds I felt Bindweed emerging from my pocket and scurrying up my dress until she got to my shoulder. She reached out. I thought she might be going to poke me, but she touched my cheek very gently. It was already damp.

'You're crying,' she said.

'Just a little bit,' I mumbled. 'Keep your voice down. Mum and Robin are just outside. They might hear.'

'What's the matter?' Bindweed whispered right into my ear.

'Nothing. I'm simply being silly,' I said.

'Don't you want to go and see these dinosaurs, whatever they are?' Bindweed asked.

'It's not that. It's Dad,' I said thickly, blowing my nose on a piece of toilet paper.

'But you haven't got this dad any more,' said Bindweed.

'I know. But I still miss him,' I said.

'Why?' Bindweed persisted.

'Because I suppose I still love him,' I said. 'I know it's silly, but I wish wish wish I could see him again. Didn't you love your father?'

'I didn't ever know him,' said Bindweed, sounding surprised. 'Fairies don't live in families. I think my mother stayed until I flowered, but I can't say I remember her. Fairies don't waste time on relationships. We might mate occasionally on a whim, but then we go our separate ways. We don't bother with this thing called love.'

'But love is the best thing ever,' I sniffled, thinking of Mum and Robin and me all having a cuddle together.

'It doesn't look as if it makes you happy,' said Bindweed, wiping a tear from my cheek. 'Still, I'm willing to give it a try, even though you have so far failed dismally to find me a new home.'

'Give what a try?' I asked.

Mum started knocking on the door of my cubicle. 'Mab? Are you all right in there?' she called anxiously.

'Yes, Mum, I'm fine,' I said, trying to stuff Bindweed back inside my pocket. It was difficult because she'd spread her wings for some reason and had puffed herself up until she looked unusually plump.

I scrubbed my face dry with toilet paper and then came out of the cubicle. Mum took one look at me and gave me a hug. I normally feel really embarrassed if Mum hugs me in

public now, but this time I gave her a big hug back.

'Let me into the hug too,' said Robin, wriggling between us.

'Careful!' I said, worried about Bindweed.

'Does your tummy still hurt then?' Mum asked.

'No, it's just a bit of a squash,' I said.

'Tyrone doesn't mind being squashed. He squashes back. And he bites,' said Robin, making his dinosaur attack Mum and me.

'Tell him to calm down or we won't take him to see his very big brothers,' I said.

'Come on then,' said Mum.

The dinosaurs were incredible, much more realistic than I'd imagined, though the gallery was so crowded you had to peer round people to get a glimpse of them. You could certainly hear them, though there was a general hubbub and several screams.

'I can't *see!*' Robin said, so Mum picked him up.

'There's a little boy over there crying!' said Robin scornfully. It was a relief to find he didn't seem a bit frightened of the dinosaurs. He happily held Tyrone up to wave to them. But when two of the dinosaurs seemed to be attacking another one on the ground, Robin suddenly burst into tears himself.

'They're *hurting* it!' he said. 'Make them stop!'

'Ah, bless!' said a grandma who was trying to control several over-excited little children herself.

She'd turned round to look at Robin, creating a chink in the crowd, so I could see a family peering at the next dinosaur along. The man had a very little boy – not much more than a baby – hoisted onto his shoulders. He had a blond lady cuddled up to him, who looked a bit like Mum, but younger and prettier. She had a girl beside her, about my age or a bit younger, who was wearing a really cool T-shirt of a lion roaring, exactly like one I'd wanted. She said something and the man laughed and gave her shoulder a fond squeeze.

My own shoulder tingled. Dad used to squeeze my shoulder like that. I narrowed my eyes, peering at the man. He had golden hair, the same colour as Dad's – but it was cut quite short, whereas my dad had lovely hair right down to his shoulders. He wasn't wearing the sort of things Dad wore either. I vividly remembered his dark velvet jackets, odd patterned trousers, rainbow-striped boots, magical clothes. This man was wearing ordinary jeans and a blue T-shirt and white trainers, like millions of other dads – and yet I stared at him, hypnotized.

Was he my dad, even though he didn't look like him at all? I kept blinking, convinced I was imagining him, but he didn't disappear. Then something made him turn round, a little awkwardly because of the child on his shoulders. He looked through the crowd and saw me.

He stared. He had my dad's blue eyes. It *was* him, beyond any doubt.

Mum sensed I'd gone very still.

'What's up, Mab? You're not fussed by the dinosaurs, are you, darling?' she asked. Then she looked the way I was peering. She suddenly gripped my hand. 'Oh my God!' she murmured, and then she plunged through the crowd towards him.

'Mum! Come back! The dinosaurs will get you!' Robin cried, panicking.

Several grown-ups chuckled and the grandma bent to comfort him, but Robin struggled free and burrowed his way towards Mum. I followed them, feeling sick. I prayed Mum would veer away when she saw the blond woman and the children with Dad, but she didn't even seem to notice them.

'Jonny!' she called shrilly. I could hear her above the roar of the dinosaurs and the buzz of the crowd. 'Jonny!'

I saw Dad's head jerk violently, almost unbalancing the

little boy, who protested and clutched his short hair. Dad looked as if he was trying to get away, but the crowd was too thick and Mum too determined. She barged her way through until she was right in front of him.

'Oh, Mum!' I whispered. I remembered the days after Dad walked out on us. The days when she cried constantly, the days when she lay in bed with the sheets over her head, the day when she didn't flinch even when I shook her and shouted in her ear and I had to phone for help. Now it might happen all over again. And it was all my fault.

It was as if I could hear my own voice now, wish wish wishing. I tried to yank Bindweed out of my pocket to get her to make Dad and this new family disappear, not even caring if anyone spotted her, but she was lying limply like a paper doll. Her eyes fluttered but she seemed genuinely in a faint. I thrust her back and elbowed my way towards Dad.

Mum was right up close to him, saying his name over and over. Robin was hanging onto her top, trying to pull her away. The dinosaurs loomed large in front of them, roaring. The pretty blond lady was helping her little boy off Dad's shoulders and lifting him down. The girl was peering at Mum, shaking her head at her.

'Who's that lady? How does she know Dad?' she asked her own mother.

'I think she's got mixed up. She's mistaken Dad for someone else,' she said.

'She's not mistaken!' I cried. 'He's *our* dad. Well, he used to be, until he left us.'

People weren't looking at the dinosaurs now. They were staring at us. Dad shook his head, looking appalled.

'Come on, we'd better go,' he said, trying to steer this other family towards the exit. 'I don't know why she's doing this.'

'Jonny, I just want you to explain!' Mum said desperately, taking hold of his shoulder.

He tried to push her away. He didn't hurt her, but I couldn't bear it.

'Don't treat Mum like that! Stop pretending! You know who she is. You know who I am, even though you haven't seen me for years. You *know* I'm Mab.'

He was trying to stare straight past me, but then he screwed up his face.

'Oh, Mab,' he said. 'Of course I know who you are. You're my girl.'

CHAPTER THIRTEEN

We went downstairs to the cafe, Mum and Robin and me, Dad and his new partner, Jude, and her daughter, Lucy, and their little son, Ryan. And Bindweed in my pocket. We sat at a table introducing ourselves, as if we weren't really connected at all. Then there was a silence.

I took a deep breath. 'Thank you for my birthday card, Dad,' I said.

He looked a bit startled. Then he nodded. 'Ah! OK. Glad you liked it.'

I knew right away he was bluffing. He hadn't sent the

card, or any of the ones before. It looked like Mum had been pretending to be him. I'd sometimes wondered.

Robin couldn't work anything out. He glared at Ryan, who was sitting on Dad's lap, as there weren't enough chairs for everyone.

'Why does that boy get to sit on Dad's lap?' he asked me.

'Because he's Dad's little boy,' I said.

'*I'm* his boy, aren't I?' said Robin.

'Yes, but Ryan is too. He's our half-brother,' I said.

Robin peered at him uneasily, as if he was only half a boy. 'So she's our half-sister?' he said, nodding at Lucy. She was sitting very close to her mother, glaring at us.

'No, I think she's Dad's stepdaughter,' I said. 'That's right, isn't it, Mum?'

Mum shrugged vaguely. She seemed in a daze, staring at Dad. 'Why did you cut your hair?' she murmured.

It seemed an odd thing to ask first. Surely she should be demanding why Dad left us, why he got together with Jude, why he didn't explain, why he preferred her to Mum, why he'd had a little boy when he already had Robin, and why, oh why, did he want to live with someone else's daughter when he already had *me*?

Lucy saw me staring and poked the tip of her tongue out at me. Not enough for anyone else to notice but me. It was the sly sort of thing Cathy would do. She wanted me to poke my tongue out too and everyone would see, so I'd be the one who got told off.

Dad ran his fingers through his short hair self-consciously. 'I was looking a bit of an old hippy,' he said. He glanced at Jude. Perhaps it was her idea.

'It isn't right for your music though,' said Mum.

'Yeah, well, I don't play any more. Not now . . .' He gestured towards his new family.

'You gave up your music?' Mum said, sounding shocked. 'So what do you do now?'

'Well, I work in a jeans shop,' said Dad.

'It's where we met, isn't it?' said Jude. She reached out and put her hand over his. She was wearing a ring on her third finger. It was a big silver band, not a gold wedding ring, but it was clear she was showing us he belonged to her. She looked over at us. 'So these are *your* kids, Jonny?' she said. 'I thought you said you were only with this Liz a couple of years?'

Dad looked shifty. 'Well, I suppose it was a bit more than that. But we were never married.'

Mum looked as if he'd slapped her. 'Because you said you didn't need a piece of paper to show the world how much you loved me,' she said shakily. 'We have two children. Did you never think how they'd feel when you just walked out the door and disappeared?'

'Look, they were only little. I'm sorry. I thought it would be easier if I went off without any fuss,' said Dad.

'Easier for you,' said Mum.

'Well, it's all water under the bridge now,' said Dad. He passed round the big plate of cakes he'd bought. They were slices of coffee and walnut, my favourite, but I knew even one bite would make me sick. I had a few sips of the elderflower pressé I'd asked for because I'd never had one and it sounded lovely. I thought Bindweed would like it, though I didn't know how I'd manage to give her a sip.

She seemed to have perked up a little and was peeping over the top of my pocket. Had she really granted my wish and somehow made Dad and this new family appear as if by magic? Because, if it *was* magic, maybe it wasn't my real dad, and maybe Jude and Lucy and Ryan didn't even exist. They were made-up people that she'd brought to life, the way Robin made up Fido.

The adults were all staring at each other. I quickly reached out and gave Lucy's arm a poke.

'Ow!' she said and rubbed her arm furiously.

She felt real, sadly.

'What's the matter, Lucy?' her mum asked.

'That girl poked me!' she said. 'Look! It's gone all red.'

It had only been a tiny poke but it had left a little mark.

'*I* didn't poke her!' I said.

Robin's eyes widened. He must have seen me.

'Don't be silly, dear,' Mum said to Lucy. She made the word *dear* sound like an insult. 'Mab would never poke anyone. She's not that kind of girl.'

'She *did* poke and it hurt a *lot*!' said Lucy in a whiny voice.

'No she didn't!' said Robin. 'You poked yourself!'

I felt so touched that he was fibbing for me.

'Come on now. Stop squabbling, kids,' said Dad. 'Look, this doesn't have to be a big deal, does it? I didn't want this to happen but, now it has, let's make it work. It's good that you kids can meet each other, seeing as you're kind of relatives.'

'No we're not,' said Lucy. 'They're not anything to do with me.'

'OK, Luce, but Ryan is,' said Dad.

Ryan looked bewildered and started to cry.

'Hey, hey, no grizzles – you're my big boy,' said Dad.

'*I'm* your big boy!' said Robin.

'Yes, you are, pal. You've grown so much! So come on, tell me all about yourself,' said Dad. 'What do you like?'

'I like dinosaurs,' said Robin.

'And . . . ?'

'Just dinosaurs,' said Robin, shrugging.

'Oh, come on, what else? Football? Music? Ryan here's got a toy piano and he can pick out a little tune already, can't you, Ry?'

'I like all them things and I can play a real piano and

I'm going to give a big concert and go on television,' Robin blurted out.

'Really?' said Dad. 'Come off it, mate! You're having me on, aren't you?'

'Leave him alone,' I said. 'Can't you see he's just trying to impress you.'

'Sorry, sorry. So what about you, Mab?'

'Is she really called *Mab*?' Jude asked Dad.

'It's a lovely name,' I said, though I'd always hated it. 'It's the name of the Queen of the Fairies.'

'You're not into all that fairy stuff like your mum, are you?' Dad asked.

I flinched. 'Yes, I am. I'm actually doing a project about fairies at school,' I said.

'You don't believe in fairies, do you – a big girl like you!' said Jude, and Lucy sniggered.

'Yes, I do,' I said firmly.

'Oh, Liz, have you filled her up with all that rubbish? Do you want to turn her into a laughing stock at school?' said Dad.

Mum had tears in her eyes. 'She's doing really well at school. Top of the class. And very artistic. She's a girl to be proud of. Both the kids are.'

'That's great,' said Dad. He gave me a silly thumbs-up sign. Lucy glared. 'You're great kids too,' he said to her, and he gave Ryan's nose a funny little tweak.

I hated watching. It was obvious that he loved them far more than us. Plus he loved this Jude far more than Mum. He was looking at Mum with his eyes creased up as if he couldn't believe he was once her partner.

I'd seen photos of the two of them together. She looked so much younger then. She didn't have those sharp lines on her face. Her hair was much fairer and came right down to her waist. She was much prettier than Jude then. But then she got ill, and anxious, and even though she was so much better now, she still always worried about everything. Worried they'd take us away again.

'Mum's not been well,' I blurted out.

'Mab!' said Mum. 'Don't.'

'She had a breakdown because you left, Dad,' I said.

He shifted awkwardly. 'Well, you've always been bothered with your nerves, haven't you, Liz,' he said.

'I suppose,' she said, though she was shaking her head, looking dazed.

'No she hasn't. We were happy together once. I can

 242

remember,' I said. We *had* been happy, hadn't we? I thought of those walks to the swings, the times we went to the seaside and had fish and chips, the summer fairs when we all went barefoot in the grass, the Christmases when we opened our presents in Mum and Dad's bed.

'I can remember too,' said Robin, making Tyrone walk along the table top with his weird long feet. 'And so can my dinosaur,' he added, though he'd only had him about an hour. He suddenly made Tyrone spring into the air and land on Dad's wrist as he tried handing round the cake plate again. The dinosaur's hard little head banged against Dad's flesh as if he was biting it.

'Hey, stop it, Robin – that hurts!' said Dad.

'It's not me – it's Tyrone,' said Robin.

Dad looked at Mum. 'Is he a bit . . . backward?'

'No, he's not!' Mum said, snapping into herself again. 'He's very bright. He's simply very imaginative.' She leaned forward. 'These are your *children*, Jon.'

'No we're not. Not any more,' I said.

'I think you're right, Mab,' Mum said suddenly. She stood up. 'Come on, you two. We're going.'

'Don't go now, Liz! We're just getting to know each

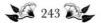

other again, the kids and me,' said Dad, though he looked relieved.

'Let her go if she wants,' said Jude. 'This is so awkward!'

'Is that what you think it is – *awkward*?' said Mum, staring at her.

'Well, it is for me! What's this whole situation like for me and *my* kids? Up till now I thought you were simply some dippy girlfriend in Jonny's past. I didn't realize there were kids involved. You're not the only one who's got a right to be upset, you know!' she said. 'Jonny's my partner now.'

'Yes, and you're welcome to him,' said Mum. She took Robin's hand. 'Come on, Mab.'

I was having one more look at this dad who didn't really seem like he was my dad at all.

'Hang on. Are you still at that same address, Liz? I want to keep in touch with the kids,' he said.

'We had to move. And we've moved on too,' said Mum.

We walked out together, Mum and Robin and me. I looked back once, as we went out of the cafe. Jude was looking angry, clearly having a go at Dad. He didn't look too concerned. He was calmly eating a big slice of cake.

We hadn't finished looking at the dinosaurs, but we

couldn't bear the thought of going back in case Dad and his new family went back to the exhibition too. We hurried out of the museum. Robin hung onto Mum with one arm, and I took the other arm. She walked so quickly we had to trot. She was pressing her lips together so hard her mouth almost disappeared.

'Mum?' I said. 'What shall we do now? Shall we find a McDonald's and have lunch?' I said, though I wasn't the slightest bit hungry. I hoped it would cheer Robin up a little. He was always desperate to go to McDonald's.

'I think maybe we should just go home,' said Mum. 'I'm looking for the bus stop. Oh, there it is! Look, a bus is coming. Quick!'

She rushed forward to join the queue, and we ran too, and managed to jump on in time. By the time we'd climbed up to the top of the bus Mum was so breathless she could hardly speak.

Robin and I sat either side of her, peering at her anxiously.

'Mum?' I said again. 'Oh, please, please, please don't be too upset.'

'I'm all right, darling. You mustn't worry about me,' Mum said jerkily, barely able to speak.

'I can't help worrying,' I said.

'Oh, Mab, you poor love,' Mum said, and put her arm round me. 'I've been such a useless mum.'

'You're a lovely mum. It's Dad who's useless,' I said fiercely.

'No, he was a good father in his way,' said Mum. 'While he was with us. But I can't get over how different he is now.'

'I don't think that man in the museum was my *real* dad,' Robin said. He squashed right up to Mum and wriggled onto her lap. 'I'm glad Tyrone bit him. Oh no! Where's Tyrone?'

'Oh, darling, you must have dropped him,' said Mum. She clutched Robin tightly. 'I'd normally go back and look for him or maybe get you another, but I just want to get right away. I can't bear the thought of bumping into them again.'

'Never mind,' said Robin, making a huge effort. 'I'm not sure I like dinosaurs any more.'

'I don't either,' I said. I kept thinking of Dad with that little boy on his shoulders, making such a fuss of him. And Dad putting his arm round that girl who wasn't even his own daughter.

I stared out of the window to distract myself. My eyes had gone watery so all I saw was a blur of green. I thought it was Kensington Gardens again but when I blinked hard I saw it

wasn't a park. It was a big cemetery with gravestones all over the grass. It was all a little wild and tangled around the edges, with ivy growing over some of the graves and white flowers rioting in the hedges.

'Is that bindweed?' I whispered.

There was a stirring in my pocket. Bindweed poked her head right out, but she was too low down to see out of the window. She tried scrambling out altogether just as Mum looked round. I clamped my hand down on top of her. She screamed at me, but luckily Mum was too distracted to notice.

'Oh no!' she said. 'I think we're going the wrong way. Dear goodness, I'm such a fool. Come on, darlings, we've got to get off again.'

I hoped the bus stop was right next to the cemetery, but by the time we'd staggered back down the stairs and remembered to ring the bell, we'd been driven way up the road.

'How could I have been so silly!' said Mum. 'It's the shock. I still can't believe that actually happened. It's like it was a dream.'

'A bad dream,' said Robin. 'I didn't like that man.'

'Don't say that. He's still your father,' said Mum. Her face

was screwed up and she rubbed the back of her neck. 'But he didn't really seem like the man he used to be. He looks so . . . ordinary now. Still, I look different too.'

'You look lovely, Mum,' I said, as we crossed over to the bus stop on the other side of the road. Bindweed was still squashed in my hand, struggling to free herself. I stuck her back in my pocket but kept my hand over her, just in case.

'Mum, I don't suppose we could walk back a bit? There was a cemetery there and I'd love to go and walk around it,' I said, trying to sound as casual as I could.

'You want to go to a cemetery, darling?' Mum said. 'What on earth for?'

'Well, I – I just liked the look of it,' I said. 'I want to look at the gravestones.'

'That's a bit morbid, isn't it?' said Mum. 'Maybe we'll go another time. I need to get home now. I'm starting to get one of my headaches.'

She was very pale, and I could see little beads of sweat on her forehead. My tummy started churning. Mum had had a whole series of headaches when she started to get ill before. Was the shock of seeing Dad going to make her ill all over again?

'Oh, Mum,' I said. 'Look, lean against the wall. Have you got any headache pills in your bag? Don't worry, we'll get you home.'

I patted her as reassuringly as I could. I shouldn't have taken my hand out of my pocket. Bindweed burst out of it and flew up in the air. I gasped. They'd see her! But Mum had her eyes screwed up, hating the dazzle of the sun, and Robin had his head bent, walking up and down the pavement trying not to tread on any lines.

'Come back!' I whispered urgently, trying to catch Bindweed.

She dodged upwards, out of my reach. 'I need to go and find the place with bindweed!' she called. The traffic was so noisy she could scarcely be heard.

'No! Don't go! Not yet! I'll take you!' I whispered.

But she was flying away now, without a backward glance. She hadn't even said goodbye. I watched her, tears spilling down my cheeks.

'Don't cry, Mab,' said Robin, coming back to me.

'Dad really wasn't nice.'

'I know,' I said, wiping my eyes with the back of my hand.

I could hardly see Bindweed now, just a distant shimmer as she flapped her wings. She was flying lower down, almost skimming the heads of passers-by. Then lower still – and then she suddenly dropped right to the pavement. She lay there, not moving, while people carried on walking in their hard shoes.

'Stay with Mum!' I told Robin urgently, and I tore down the road towards Bindweed.

CHAPTER FOURTEEN

I saw men with polished lace-ups, women with pointy high heels, teenagers with Docs, all of them stamping along, none of them looking down at the pavement.

'Watch out!' I bellowed. 'Don't tread on her!'

People stared at me nervously, and a lady tried to stop me to see if she could help, but I pulled away from her and went on running. I reached Bindweed, bent down, and shoved her in my pocket.

'What on earth . . . ?' said the lady indignantly.

'I had to rescue my – my pet butterfly,' I stammered.

'You have a pet *butterfly*?' she repeated. 'Isn't that very cruel?'

'I wanted to set it free somewhere safe, but it just flew out of my pocket. I've got it now. I'm sorry I seemed rude. Well, I must go now,' I gabbled.

'Wait a minute!' She had hold of me again. 'Are you on your own?'

'No. I've got my mum and my brother back there,' I said. 'Please let me go!'

I twisted round to point back down the road and saw them running towards me.

'There they are!' I said, relieved.

'Mab! Oh, darling, wait!' Mum called.

She reached me and threw her arms round me. I wanted to hug her back hard, but I was mindful of Bindweed collapsed in my pocket.

'Why did you run away like that?' Mum asked.

'Did Nibbles escape from your pocket?' Robin asked.

I stared at him blankly, and then remembered I'd made up a story about an imaginary mouse.

'Yes, he did,' I said.

'Nibbles?' Mum asked.

'Her pet butterfly,' said the lady. 'Did she have it when it was a caterpillar?'

'I'm sorry?' Mum said faintly. She shook her head, trying to clear it. 'We have to go and get the bus now.'

We walked away from the baffled woman.

'Oh, Mab,' Mum murmured. She looked dreadful, even whiter now, and she kept yawning.

'Mum, you're not going to be sick, are you?' I asked.

'I hope not,' said Mum. 'What on earth was all that Nibbles nonsense about? You were trying to run back to find Dad, weren't you?'

'No!'

'It's all right – it's only natural that you want to be with him,' said Mum. 'Oh God, I think I *am* going to be sick.'

She managed to run down a little alleyway and was sick into the gutter while we watched helplessly.

'Poor Mum,' said Robin. 'It can't have been that cake because she didn't even eat it. None of us did.'

'I'm sorry,' Mum murmured. 'I feel a bit better now.'

She didn't really look better, and when we were on the right bus she sat with her eyes closed. I didn't know what to do, with a collapsed mother beside me and a collapsed fairy in my pocket. I stared at the cemetery as we drove past, seeing more bindweed flowers now, but I kept quiet.

Robin was fidgeting anxiously beside us. 'Do you think Mum's going to be sick again?' he whispered.

I shook my head, hoping I was right. The bus seemed extra jerky, stopping and starting abruptly in the traffic. I started to feel sick myself. When we got off the bus at our own stop at last we had to sit inside the bus shelter until our tummies settled.

'Well, I feel fine,' said Robin. 'But I wish I still had Tyrone to play with.'

He gently took Mum's handbag from her limp grasp and peered inside. 'Could I play with your big spider instead, Mab?'

'I don't really want to get it out of its cellophane box, seeing as it's a present for Micky,' I said. 'I can't wait to see his face!'

'Couldn't it be a present for me instead?' Robin asked. 'Don't you like me more than Micky?'

'Yes, but you're not doing a project on arachnids,' I said.

'What are they?'

'Spiders!'

'Well, why not say so? Why call them that funny name that no one understands?' said Robin. 'You're a show-off.'

'No I'm not! You're simply a little squirt who doesn't know anything yet,' I said.

'Children! Stop squabbling,' Mum said weakly. 'What's the matter with you?'

It was a silly question. We'd all been knocked sideways meeting Dad. I was especially worried about Mum. She wasn't sick again, but when we got home she couldn't even face a cup of tea. I went to my bedroom and fished Bindweed out of my pocket. I laid her out gently in the palm of my hand and peered at her closely. She was still very limp but she opened her eyes wearily.

'Oh, Bindweed, you really frightened me when you flew off like that,' I whispered. 'Are you all right now?'

'Do I look all right?' Bindweed snapped.

'Sorry! I'm just so worried about you. And Mum. I'm so scared she's going to get ill again. It's all gone so wrong. Dad doesn't want us any more and Mum can't bear it,' I said, starting to cry. Tears started streaming down my face.

'Mind out, you're splashing me!' said Bindweed.

I wiped my eyes with my free hand, trying to force myself to stop crying. I choked back my next sob and made a weird snorty sound instead.

'Really!' said Bindweed, but she stood up on my hand and dried another tear with the hem of her white frock. 'Why do humans have to *care* so much? It seems so painful.'

'I suppose we can't help it,' I said, sniffling. 'I wish poor Mum didn't care so much about Dad.'

Mum called to me from the kitchen. 'I've made beans on toast for a late lunch, Mab. Come and eat it before it gets cold.'

'Shall I bring you a little portion, Bindweed?' I asked.

'Beans?' said Bindweed. 'Green pointy vegetation?' She looked hopeful.

'Well, these will be little round soft beans in an orange sauce,' I said. 'And toast is only bread but a bit burnt.'

'No, thank you,' Bindweed said, shuddering. 'I don't care for anything orange or charred. Please put me in my bed to recuperate.'

'Recuperate?'

'To recover,' Bindweed said, yawning. 'A freshly opened bud has more command of vocabulary than you. Besides, I have work to do.'

'What work?' I asked, as I tucked her up in the slipper.

But Mum was calling again and I had to go to her. She'd made beans and toast for Robin and me, but didn't have any herself. She simply sipped a cup of tea, looking exhausted.

'Why don't you go and have a lie-down, Mum?' I said. 'You need to recuperate.'

'I need to what?' said Mum. 'You and your fancy words, Mab!' She was holding her head, massaging it with her fingers.

'Is your headache really bad?' I asked.

'My head doesn't really hurt any more. It just feels . . . funny.' She stifled a yawn.

'Do go to bed, Mum. Robin and I will be fine, honestly,' I said.

'Well, I will have a little nap if that's all right,' Mum said. 'Wake me up in twenty minutes – promise?'

'OK. Off you go then,' I said.

'I do love you so, Mab,' said Mum. 'And you, Robin. And . . .' She shook her head, looking puzzled, as she went to her bedroom.

'Mum *will* be all right?' Robin asked me anxiously, as he ran his finger round the sauce left on his plate.

'Don't do that! Yes, Mum's just a bit sleepy – that's all,' I said, trying to sound convincing. 'Help me wash up and then we'll watch a film, all right?'

'I could lick the plates clean,' said Robin, semi-seriously.

'As if we want your mucky lick all over our plates!' I said. 'Take them over to the sink. Which film do you want to watch?'

'Anything. But not a dinosaur one,' said Robin.

We settled down on the sofa to watch *A Hundred and One Dalmatians* for probably the one hundred and first time. Robin clutched Fido so he could watch it too. After a while I went to the bedroom to check on Mum. She was sprawled on her back, her shoes kicked off but otherwise fully dressed. She was breathing deeply, and looked so peaceful I felt it would be unfair to wake her up.

I left her sleeping and went into my own room. I looked at Bindweed, but she was sleeping too, so pale and still she looked like a little wax fairy. I didn't have the heart to wake her either.

I curled up in my own bed and cried for a little while, wondering if Mum's illness was starting all over again. Would Robin and I have to be fostered once more? I remembered that foster mum and dad who looked after us – for nearly a whole year! They were kind and let us sleep in the same bed as each other and they gave us an ice cream if we started crying, but I didn't like them because they weren't Mum, they weren't Dad. Their house smelled funny and their food didn't taste right, not even the ice cream.

I knew I wouldn't be allowed to look after Robin in our own house, but I thought it bitterly unfair. I was much older

now and I knew exactly what to do. I was like a second mother to him – everyone said so, even Mum herself.

I wanted to stay cuddled up under my duvet but I made myself get up, wash my face, and go into the living room. Robin was on the sofa with his arms round Fido, still watching *A Hundred and One Dalmatians*. He'd pulled Fido's ears right over his button eyes.

'This is the scary bit and I didn't want him to get upset,' said Robin. He sounded a little scared himself.

'But you know it all turns out happily,' I said.

'I know, but maybe one time it won't,' said Robin.

'Like meeting Dad,' I said.

'Mm,' said Robin. 'Ssh, now. I'm watching the film.'

I was happy not to discuss Dad too. I kept thinking about that girl Lucy. She was prettier than me. And cuter. A Cathy sort of girl. Dad seemed to like her an awful lot. As if she was his real daughter and not me.

I nestled close to Robin and watched the film with him, and then we watched *Frozen*, though we could both chant it backwards. When we got to the part when Elsa sings 'Let It Go', we rewound it and sang along together. Then another voice joined in, a lovely sweet voice, and Mum came into the

living room singing away, even doing all the right gestures. Her eyes were a bit puffy but she'd brushed her hair and changed into her blue frock – it was old and faded now, but it still really suited her.

'Thank you for letting me have that nap, darlings. I feel much better now,' she said, sitting on the sofa with us. 'The headache's nearly gone.'

'Are you really all right, Mum?' I asked.

'Yes, I am,' she said. She suddenly squeezed me tight. 'Truly all right. I'm not getting ill again, I promise. I'm so sorry I put you through all that before.'

'You couldn't help it. The doctor explained,' I said.

'Well, anyway, I'm better now,' said Mum.

'Ssh! We're missing the *film*,' said Robin.

Mum ruffled his hair. 'Sorry, Your Lordship!'

She let us have pizza for tea. I wasn't sure it would appeal to Bindweed, so while it was heating up I asked if I could have some salad first.

'Of course, darling. Very good for you,' said Mum. She went to get up.

'No, I'll do it, Mum. You stay sitting and have your cup of tea,' I said.

I chopped up a stub of cucumber and a lettuce leaf, put them in a tiny cup and went into my bedroom. I put it under the bed beside Bindweed in her slipper, with another thimbleful of water.

'Bindweed!' I whispered. 'Wake up!'

She didn't stir. I started to get frightened.

'Bindweed! Come on! Supper!' I said sharply.

She stuck her head out of the slipper, her cap askew. 'Do you have to call me like that? I'm not your pet dog, you know,' she said.

'No, you're my pet fairy, and that's far more special,' I said, sitting down cross-legged on the carpet beside her.

She glared at me but crawled slowly out of the slipper. Her wings were crushed, but when she wriggled her shoulders they sprang out like tiny translucent umbrellas. 'Thank goodness,' she murmured. 'I thought they might have permanently lost power.'

'Well, you shouldn't have tried to fly away from me like that! It was so dangerous. Anyone could have snatched at you when you were airborne – and when you fell to the floor you very nearly got trodden on,' I said.

'Don't talk to me like one of your teachers!' said Bindweed,

seizing the thimble and drinking from it thirstily. 'You forget I'm nearly two hundred years older than you and surely deserve a little respect. And I'm an expert flier. In former days folk marvelled at my long-distance flying. I have even made an ocean crossing.'

'You've flown over the *ocean*?' I said incredulously.

'With a little help from a seagull,' she said. 'And anyway, of course I flew away. I wanted to see this cemetery where you saw bindweed. You did see it, didn't you? You weren't just playing a trick on me to torment me?'

'I wouldn't do that! But I couldn't go there, not when Mum was feeling so ill. It was such a shock seeing Dad at the museum,' I said. I hugged my knees, shivering.

Bindweed nibbled at a morsel of cucumber and then tried a mouthful of lettuce.

'Delicious!' she said, and ate on heartily.

I thought cucumber and lettuce tasted of nothing very much, but I was glad I'd managed to please her.

'I take it you didn't enjoy seeing your father,' she said.

'It was awful,' I murmured.

'There's gratitude! I am still recovering from my long incarceration, but I did my very best to grant you your wish, practically extinguishing myself with the effort – and you say the experience was *awful*!' Bindweed took another gulp of water and looked as if she was considering spitting it at me.

I wriggled further away from her, just in case. 'I know. You tried so hard, and it should have been the most wonderful thing in the whole world. But it wasn't.'

'What did you expect?' Bindweed asked.

I tried to get my thoughts clear. I suppose I'd imagined Dad standing somewhere, holding his arms out and calling my name. I'd run to him, and he'd lift me up in his arms and whirl me round and tell me how much he loved me and missed me and that I was his own special daughter. He'd make a fuss of Robin, throwing him up in the air, and then give him a bear hug, and tell him he was the best little boy in the world. Then he'd turn to Mum and they'd be like film stars, staring at each

other mesmerized, and then embrace as if they could never let each other go.

It was too embarrassing to admit this to Bindweed. Why hadn't I realized that Dad would probably have a new partner and new children too? He belonged to them now, not to us.

Bindweed watched me, eating her way through a sliver of cucumber as if it was watermelon. 'I strained my magical powers to the utmost,' she said, 'but there's a limit to what I can do. I thought it was a most tremendous feat to summon up your father and his new family out of the blue. I can't help it if your expectations were too high.' She sounded huffy, but sorrowful too. 'I truly wanted to give you a parting gift, Mab.'

'Do we really have to part?' I asked. 'I'll try to make you feel really at home here. I could make you a proper bed for a start. I'm sure I've seen fairy bowers advertised in Mum's fairy magazines. And I could ask Mum if I could cut up an old dress of mine and make a special padded shoulder purse to carry you in. It would be much comfier than a pocket or a sock. I'd make sure you got plenty of fresh air every day. And I'd take you to school again so you could sniff Mrs Horsley's roses.'

'It wouldn't be a *real* home though,' said Bindweed. 'I know you mean it kindly, Mab, but I am fully alive now, not in hibernation. If I don't rewild myself soon I will simply wither and die.'

'Well, you mustn't do that! I'll see if Mum will take us on the bus again tomorrow so we can go to that big cemetery place,' I promised. 'Though it seems a bit of a weird place to want as your home, with all the dead people.'

'Wentworth had its own mausoleum,' said Bindweed, her voice faint with longing. 'It was a beautiful stone building in the gothic tradition, neglected for many years. The ivies took it over, in their ugly swarming way, but the climbing roses and the honeysuckles took their grip too, so we bindweeds slithered stealthily amongst them, choking them year by year.'

'That's not very nice,' I said. 'Couldn't you all find a special space, instead of choking each other?'

'Nature isn't "nice",' said Bindweed. 'Bindweeds don't share. They compete.'

I could see I wouldn't like Bindweed at all if she were a little girl human being. But I somehow liked her very much as an ancient fairy. I was glad I had one more night with her.

*

There didn't seem to be a good moment to bring up the idea of another trip into town that evening. I helped Mum at Robin's bath time because her head still went a bit swimmy when she bent over.

'I think I'd better have an early night tonight,' she said. She was smiling, but she was still very pale.

'You *are* all right though, Mum, aren't you?' I checked again.

'Yes, darling. I promise. I'm only tired out because of everything's that happened today,' she assured me, giving me a hug.

'And you're not too unhappy about . . . things?' I went on.

'I'm fine, darling. What about you?' Mum asked, holding me at arm's length so she could have a proper look at me.

'I'm fine too,' I said, though it wasn't quite true.

We both went to bed when Robin did. I left my bedroom door open. I listened hard but I couldn't hear anything – no tossing and turning, no sighs, no smothered crying. I hoped Mum had gone to sleep straight away. I was very tired too, but every time I closed my eyes I relived the moment when I'd seen Dad at the dinosaur exhibition, and that awful time in the cafe with him and his new family.

I dreamed it when I eventually went to sleep and woke up in the middle of the night with my head still reeling with it. I sat up in bed, trying hard to think of other things. I thought about Bindweed, the cemetery, my fairy project, Micky, Mrs Horsley, Billie, even Cathy – I didn't care what it was, I simply needed to stop stop stop thinking about Dad.

Then I heard the click of a light being switched on in the kitchen, and the watery rush of the kettle being filled. I slipped out of bed and scurried to the kitchen. There was Mum in her dressing gown. Her eyes were red, her eyelids very puffy.

'Oh, Mum!' I said, rushing to her. 'You're not fine! You're getting ill again.'

'I promise I'm not getting ill, darling. Promise, promise, promise,' said Mum, putting the kettle down and giving me a hug.

'But you've been crying!' I said. 'You're sad all over again.'

'Of course I'm sad, sweetheart. I'm sad that you worry so about me. I'd give anything in the whole world not to have gone to pieces when Dad left us. It must have been so scary for you,' Mum said. Her eyes filled with tears again. 'I hate myself for being so weak. How could I have just taken to my bed instead of looking after you two?'

'You couldn't help it. The doctor explained. It was because you were depressed,' I said, patting Mum on the back.

'I'm a terrible mother,' Mum whispered, her words almost drowned by the sound of the boiling kettle.

'No you're not! You're the best mother in the world,' I said. 'Are we having a cup of tea? Shall I make it for you?'

'I'll make it, pet,' said Mum.

'What about Robin?' I asked, getting out the cups.

'He's fast asleep. This is just a girls-only midnight feast,' said Mum, taking a couple of teacakes out of the tin.

'Oh, yum!'

We sat down at the kitchen table with our cups and teacakes. I ate mine the best way, nibbling all the chocolate off first and then licking the mallow part as if it was an ice cream.

'Mucky pup,' said Mum fondly. 'Oh, Mab, I've been such

a fool. I've wasted so much time feeling sad about Dad, wishing and wishing he'd come back.'

'He didn't really send that birthday card, did he?' I said.

Mum bit her lip. Then she sighed. 'No. I pretended he did. I wanted you to think he still cares about you. And I think he does, truly. It's just he's not very good at remembering special days. He wasn't even when we were all together. He was always too busy with his music. Yet he doesn't even seem to care about that any more,' Mum said, shaking her head. 'He's so different now.'

'He's horrible,' I said.

'No he's not. He's just – ordinary. Not at all how he used to be. Or maybe he's exactly the same, and I simply thought the world of him when he was with us, when he was actually ordinary then too, in spite of his lovely hair and his clothes.'

'Maybe he put a spell on you,' I said.

'Maybe he did,' said Mum.

'But we're better off without him now, aren't we?' I said.

'Yes, we are,' said Mum, as if she really meant it.

'Perhaps someday you'll start dating again,' I said.

Mum made a scoffing sound. 'I think my dating days are over, lovie.'

'No they're not. You could go on one of those dating apps. That's how Billie's mum met Billie's stepdad,' I said.

'No thanks!' said Mum. 'I wouldn't have the nerve.'

'Well, you might meet someone without really meaning to. Someone might come into your shop and fall for you,' I said.

'Oh yes, very likely!' said Mum.

'Mr Henry might even ask you out!' I said. It was a joke to make her laugh but to my astonishment Mum blushed.

'*Mum!* Do you fancy Mr Henry?'

'No, of course not!' Mum protested. 'Though I've discovered he's actually very nice now I've got to know him. But he's my boss!'

'Does that matter? Oh, Mum, is he married?'

'*No!* He's been divorced a few years now. He did actually ask me if I had a husband or partner,' said Mum.

'And what did you say?'

'I said we were temporarily separated,' said Mum.

'*Temporarily?*'

'Well, I always hoped your dad would come back.'

'But he's not going to come back now, is he?' I said.

'No, he's not. I'm not sure I really want him to any more.

He shouldn't have walked out on us like that,' said Mum. 'And I shouldn't have gone to pieces.' She looked down, tracing the ring of fairies painted on her cup with her finger. 'All those silly wishes,' she murmured.

'Mum, *I* wish we could go on that bus ride again tomorrow and find that big cemetery again,' I said.

Mum looked at me. 'What?'

'You know. We went past it on the bus when we were going the wrong way by mistake. It's a few roads past the dinosaur museum,' I said.

'Mab, I'm not going to take you back to that museum. Dad won't be there again, darling,' Mum said, misunderstanding.

'I know. I don't want to see him or go to the museum. I want to go to the cemetery. Please!' I begged. 'You said you'd take me another time.'

'Did I?' said Mum. 'Well, maybe I will. But not tomorrow. I couldn't face another long bus ride into town, especially not the exact same route. I think we need a quiet day at home, the three of us.'

'Oh!' I said. 'So when could we go? The day after?'

'Don't be silly – it's school on Monday,' said Mum.

'Couldn't we go after school?' I persisted. I knew it was

getting urgent. Bindweed was getting weaker by the day. 'Please, Mum. I so badly need to go there. Please, please, please!'

I was used to Mum saying yes to anything I wanted, because she was so desperate to make us happy. But now she stood firm.

'Sorry, darling. It's just not practical. It would probably upset all of us. Now, stop looking at me with those great big pleading eyes! Finish your tea, and then I'll tuck you back into bed,' Mum said.

'And are you going to go back to bed too?' I asked.

'Of course,' said Mum. 'You mustn't worry so about me, Mab. I'm going to be fine now, I promise.'

I drank my last mouthful and stood up. We went into my bedroom. Mum switched on the light so she could remake my rumpled bed, smoothing my sheets and plumping up my pillow. I ducked down quickly and peeped at Bindweed. I saw her stir slightly, but she looked so frail, almost transparent. I *had* to try and find her a home. I couldn't leave it any longer.

'In you get, darling,' said Mum.

I did as I was told, and when Mum bent to kiss me I pulled her closer to whisper right in her ear.

'Mum, if I told you a secret would you absolutely swear not to tell anyone else, ever?' I breathed.

I felt Mum stiffen. 'What secret, Mab?'

'You promise you won't tell anyone at all? Not even Robin, because he wouldn't be able to keep it to himself,' I whispered.

'I promise,' said Mum.

'Well . . . I know for a fact there really are fairies,' I said.

I felt Mum relax. 'Of course there are, darling,' she said.

'Real ones. I know, because I've met one!'

'*Have* you, sweetheart?' Mum said. She sounded like she was talking to a three-year-old. She didn't believe me.

'No, I have, really. Only she's kind of fading away, because she needs to live out in the open where it's all green and wild. Somewhere very quiet, where hardly any people go, so they won't spot her,' I went on.

Mum stood up, rubbing her back. 'Somewhere like a cemetery?' she said.

'Yes!'

'Nice try, Mab. But I told you, we're not going all the way back there tomorrow. I really don't know why you're so obsessed with cemeteries! Now, settle down, lovie, there's a good girl,' said Mum.

'There really is a fairy,' I said.

'Yes, yes, a lovely fairy,' said Mum.

'I thought you of all people would believe me!'

'Maybe I've believed in too many fairies,' said Mum. 'Perhaps it's time I grew out of it.'

'No! You've got to stay believing. It's who you are. Look, I'll *show* you her, if you still promise you won't tell, or report it to the *Fairy* magazine people, or tweet about it or whatever.' I scrambled back out of bed and bent down. I felt for the slipper and then cautiously brought it out into the light, shading it so that Bindweed wouldn't be dazzled.

'Here she is!' I said softly.

Mum looked. 'Oh yes! I think I see her. She's very pretty,' she said. She sounded as if she was simply playing a game. She didn't sound the slightest bit startled.

I peered at my slipper. I couldn't see Bindweed! She must have burrowed right down inside so that she was hidden.

'It's all right, Bindweed. You can come out. Mum won't tell, she's promised,' I said, feeling for her with my finger.

She seemed to have curled up right at the very bottom of the slipper. I tipped it up and gently shook it. I waited for her to tumble out and be cross with me, but nothing happened.

 274

I looked right inside the slipper. There was no sign of her.

I'd simply got the wrong slipper! I felt for the other one, shaking my head at my own stupidity, and tried again – but that slipper was empty too.

'She's not there!' I said.

'Oh dear, she must have flown away!' said Mum.

She still didn't believe a word I was saying. She was acting the way she did with Robin and Fido. It was infuriating. I wasn't playing baby games!

'Back into bed,' said Mum. 'Night night now, darling.'

'Night, Mum,' I said, giving up.

She switched the light out and tiptoed off to her own bedroom. I lay flat on my back, waiting . . .

CHAPTER FIFTEEN

After a full five minutes I heard a tiny scampering underneath my bed, and then the slightest rustle as a very small someone climbed back inside the slipper.

I shot out of bed and grabbed it. I couldn't see in the dark, but I felt Bindweed's long curls and her little green cap.

'You hid from her!' I said.

'Of course I did,' she said, coughing. 'It's very dusty behind your bed! I daresay I'm filthy dirty now, when I always take such pains to stay pristine. I'd demand a bath in rainwater, but I'm so exhausted I'd probably drown in it. How dare you betray me!'

'It was just so that Mum would take us to that big cemetery. I was trying to help! And I made Mum promise not to tell,' I protested. 'She wouldn't ever break a promise.'

'*You* broke your promise to me!' said Bindweed. 'I've a good mind to teach you a lesson. You'll feel very silly if I magic a great big wart on the end of your nose!'

'Please don't!' I said.

'I'm very tempted,' said Bindweed. 'But it would take the little strength I have left.'

'I was only trying to help you,' I said.

'Then if you really want to help me, get back out of bed and take me to this cemetery now!' Bindweed commanded.

'I can't take you now, in the middle of the night! There aren't any buses for a start, and I don't have a card for the fare anyway. Plus, it's scary in the dark,' I said.

'I like the dark,' said Bindweed. 'I can't bear that bright light your mother switched on. What sort of a mother tries to blind you?'

'She's the best mother in the world!' I said hotly.

'You must have thought you had the best father in the world if you wanted to see him so badly,' said Bindweed.

'You'll be telling me that the girl Cathy is the best child in all the world next.'

'Mum *is* the best mother. I do wish you'd let her see you. It would have meant so much to her,' I said.

'Really? I think she'd be disappointed. I'm not at my best at the moment,' said Bindweed, running her pointy fingers through her bedraggled curls then trying to fluff out her waxy white dress, which was now very crumpled and grubby. 'Anyway, I don't remotely resemble those dinky figurines decked around your home. They're *her* idea of fairy folk.'

'Tell me more about real fairies,' I said, reaching down and picking up the slipper. I flew it up onto the bed as if it was a toy aeroplane and settled it beside me on the pillow.

She told me more about fairies – and goblins and silkies and boggarts. I wanted to get up and take further notes for my project, but I was getting very sleepy now. I couldn't keep my eyes open any longer. I dreamed of all these weird magical creatures and woke with a start as a small unicorn leaped on me and started stamping on my chest with its hard hooves.

I tried to fight back and discovered it was only Fido banging me with his wheels.

'Woof woof, wake up, Mab! I'm hungry! I want a big juicy bone!' Robin made him say.

'Hey, watch out, Fido, you're too rough!' I said, pushing him away.

'He just wants attention! Silly old Fido!' said Robin, letting him fall back on the floor. 'Budge up, Mab, I want a cuddle. Hey, why have you got your old slipper on your pillow? Shall I chuck it on the floor too?'

'No! Careful!' I snatched it from him, catching a glimpse of Bindweed diving downwards into its depths, a tiny flurry of green and white.

'What's that fluttering thing? Is it an insect?' Robin asked, flicking his finger at the slipper.

'Stop it! You'll hurt it,' I said, holding the slipper out of his reach. 'It's only Nibbles.'

'Is Nibbles a *real* mouse?' Robin asked.

'What do you think?' I replied, putting the slipper safely out of his reach on my bedside table.

'I can't always tell what's real and what's not,' said Robin.

'Let me see if *you're* real!' I said, and I started tickling him. He wriggled and squirmed, shrieking with laughter.

'Ssh, you'll wake Mum! Is she having a lie-in?' I asked.

'Yes – she's snoring!' said Robin. 'I want her to wake up soon because I want my breakfast and so does Fido.'

'I'll make breakfast,' I said.

I decided to make Mum a special birthday breakfast, even though it wasn't her birthday for ages. I made the lovely strawberry-jam heart sandwiches. They were a little lopsided, but I put the best-shaped one on Mum's plate. I also fished out a strawberry from the jam pot and put it on a twenty-pence piece that hopefully looked like a little silver platter. I served this up to Bindweed while Robin was trying hard to spoon a strawberry out for himself, and then we gave Mum her breakfast on a tray.

Her eyes still looked a bit puffy, but they shone when she saw her special breakfast.

'Bless you, darlings,' she said, sitting up and smiling. 'Are you trying to bribe me, Mab? I'm sorry, but we're still not going on another long bus journey today. If you want to look at gravestones, why don't we go and look in a churchyard around here?'

I thought about the church down the road and round the corner. We'd been there once when they'd had a summer fete. It was a very plain building, rather like a little school. It had a

patch of grass at the front, but I couldn't remember any flowers – or any gravestones either, come to that.

'You mean the church just along from the post office?' I asked.

'No, lovie, it's too modern. But there's an old church near my supermarket. It's got a big graveyard, but it's all a bit of a tangle now. All-over ivy,' said Mum, eating her jam sandwich.

'And . . . bindweed?' I asked, trying to sound casual.

'Oh, there are lots of weeds,' said Mum. 'It doesn't look as if they've had a gardener round for donkey's years. I don't think people go there much nowadays.'

'Excellent!' I said.

'You're a funny sausage,' said Mum, shaking her head at me.

'If Mab's a sausage then Fido wants to eat her all up,' said Robin, hauling his dog up onto Mum's bed.

'Hey, hey, careful! You'll spill my tea, pet,' said Mum.

'That sounds funny, like I'm a teapet. Like a teapot, but maybe I've got a tail instead of a handle and I eat with my spout,' said Robin, laughing.

'You two are the weirdest kids in the world,' said Mum, but she laughed too.

We always had a cuddle in Mum's bed after breakfast on a Sunday. Mum would sometimes make up a story for us or we'd talk about something we'd seen on television. Mum would tell us tales about when she was a little girl. She had very strict old-fashioned parents who sometimes smacked her. Her mother tied her hair into plaits so tight she couldn't frown, and she wasn't allowed ribbons, only elastic bands. I couldn't help being glad that Granny and Grandpa weren't around any more.

She didn't just tell tales about herself. She would tell us stories about Dad when he was a little boy, and how he was always a free spirit and loved nature and animals and played music. She would remind us of the times he'd taken us for walks in the countryside and tamed birds so they landed on his hand, and played any tune we fancied on his penny whistle. I wasn't sure whether I could remember Dad doing this or not, but Mum used to make it all seem real.

Maybe it had been real, maybe it hadn't. This morning, Mum didn't mention Dad, and we didn't either. I did think about him though, wondering if he was cuddling up in bed with his new partner and her daughter and their little son. It gave me a funny pain inside.

'Have you got tummy ache, Mab?' Mum asked.

'Sort of,' I said. 'It feels . . . empty.'

'I feel a bit empty too!' said Robin. 'Let's have another breakfast!'

I wasn't feeling a really *hungry* emptiness, but it seemed a good idea all the same. Mum started to get out of bed, but I pushed her gently back on the pillows.

'No, *I'll* make it, Mum. I want to!' I said.

It gave me a chance to go and check in on Bindweed.

The strawberry had been bigger than her head but she'd eaten it all up. She looked as if she'd been garishly made up, with streaks of crimson smeared over her cheeks and round her mouth. She smacked her small lips appreciatively.

'You have kept me supplied with regular meals, some of which were scarcely edible, though I know you meant well. But this delectable strawberry is the finest I have ever eaten. Even Wentworth strawberries weren't as sweet as this one. Thank you very much, dear Mab,' she said.

It was the most grateful she had ever been, and I was very touched. 'Perhaps you'd like another?' I suggested.

'Oh, please!' she said. 'Please, please, please!'

I took her sticky twenty-pence platter and dug deep into the jam jar until I managed to find another strawberry.

'Bliss!' said Bindweed, waving her sticky hands and wriggling with joy. My slipper was going to need a good scrubbing, but I didn't really mind. I felt so fond of her now that I wished I could keep her with me for ever, but she was very pale underneath the strawberry smears. I knew I had to let her go.

'I can't be sure, but I think I've found you a new home,' I said. 'Mum says there's a graveyard nearby that's very quiet

and overgrown. It sounds as if it could be exactly the right place. We'll go there today and you can see what you think, though you'll have to have a good bath first.'

I decided it would be simplest if Bindweed joined me in my own bath. She wasn't sure she could swim, and she didn't want to get her wings wet anyway, so she rode on Robin's toy duck, sailing backwards and forwards around me while I washed myself. She trailed her hands in my soapy water and carefully washed herself, her hair and her dress, and soon she looked spotless, though very pale, and her limbs were as spindly as a spider's now.

'Oh dear, you've got so thin,' I said anxiously, peering at her.

'Yes, I definitely need feeding up,' said Bindweed, holding out her arms in front of her. 'Perhaps I might have another nibble on a strawberry?'

'I don't think there are any left in the jar,' I said. 'But I could have another scrape round just in case. Or fix you a thimbleful of the strawberry jelly part?'

'That sounds very tempting. But then I daresay I'd need to take another ride on this strange duck. Its feathers are ill-defined and it's got very silly features, but at least it doesn't

deafen with its quacking,' said Bindweed. 'The ducks on the lake at Wentworth were tremendously noisy – and the swans were exceedingly bad-tempered. A young fairy I knew tried to pluck a few small feathers to make a cloak for herself one very cold winter, and the swan struck her such a blow with its wing that she limped badly ever afterwards and couldn't rise even an inch in the air. It was very tragic.' She shook her head, tutting. 'We fairies do best if we avoid all wildlife.'

'Are you absolutely sure you want to live outside then? Wouldn't you be safer staying here with me? We aren't allowed any kind of pets in our flat. Well, Robin's got Fido, but he's not real. And I could make you your own little winter cloak – I could pull a few feathers out of my last year's puffer coat. Plus feed you strawberries every day,' I suggested, trying hard to tempt her.

Bindweed looked a little wistful but she shook her head. 'I can't speak for all fairies. I believe some species thrive in glass conservatories, but we bindweeds are wild and cannot last long indoors in captivity. I shall soon start to droop beyond revival.'

'Yet you survived being shut up in my fairy book for years and years and years,' I said.

'I was crushed into hibernation. I was in a deep sleep for

all that time, dead to the world. Bindweeds are used to this process. We die back in winter, but our roots are tenacious. We spring up again. And again and again. Ask any gardener,' said Bindweed, smiling. 'Oh, how the Wentworth gardeners used to curse us!'

'Well, it doesn't sound as if there are any gardeners at this churchyard,' I said. 'Mum says it's all covered in ivy.'

Bindweed sniffed. 'Oh dear, it sounds as if I shall be slumming it. Those ivies are so coarse and common. Still, I am so lonely now I feel I could even embrace a beastly nettle fairy.'

I couldn't help feeling hurt. I'd tried my hardest to be Bindweed's friend, but I clearly didn't count.

'Well, let's hope you can find a few wild roses to choke in this cemetery,' I said huffily.

'Oh, yes please!' said Bindweed. 'Let's go there immediately!'

I put her in my pocket without further ado and went to ask Mum.

'I think we'd better wait till later. They could be having a morning service in the church. It would look rude if we were poking around the gravestones while they were inside praying,' said Mum. 'It would be better if we went after lunch.'

Bindweed was doing some literal poking inside my pocket.

Her fingers were tiny but very sharp, and my tummy was tender.

'Ouch!' I said, wincing. 'I don't think anyone would mind. They might think we were visiting a relative. We could look very sad and holy.'

'I don't see why it's so urgent, lovie,' said Mum. 'Can't we just relax and loaf about this morning? I was thinking I might branch out and try to make a cake for tea. What sort do you fancy?'

'A *big* cake with lots of jam,' Robin suggested.

'Well, I'm not sure there's much left,' said Mum, peering in the jar. 'What about little fairy cakes with icing on the top?'

'Good plan!' said Robin. 'Ooh, I think I *like* making cakes.'

Mum looked up a recipe on the internet and started getting all the ingredients out of the cupboard. I waited to see if I had any further pokes in the stomach, but Bindweed was still. I pretended I needed to go to the bathroom so we could have a private conversation.

'*Fairy* cakes?' she said. 'Cakes specially for fairies?'

'Well, I suppose they could be. They're little cakes, though they'd seem enormous to you. I think they're very yummy, but I don't know whether you'd like them. They look

very pretty though. You can sprinkle them with hundreds and thousands.'

'Hundreds and thousands of what?' Bindweed asked.

'Tiny little sweets all different colours,' I said. 'Or you can decorate them with small silver balls – they taste good too. And *I* know, glacé cherries. I think you'd like them very much. Maybe as much as strawberries. Would you like to stay and try one?'

'Perhaps I would,' she said, licking her little lips. 'If you promise we can go to the graveyard this afternoon, with no more prevaricating.'

I wasn't sure what that meant. You really needed a dictionary handy when you had a conversation with a fairy. Still, I got Mum to promise that we would definitely go to the graveyard straight after lunch.

I suggested that Bindweed might like to take a nap in my slipper, but she said she was far too excited to sleep. She wanted to amuse herself exploring the living room while Mum and Robin and I were busy mixing and stirring in the kitchen. I imagined her peering at each fairy ornament scornfully, maybe trying out the little toadstool chairs and the small swing. She might try to get into the fairy house, though

I knew the door was stuck fast – I'd had no luck trying to poke a tiny fairy doll inside.

I couldn't see her when I popped back later into the living room when the cakes were in the oven.

'Bindweed?' I called softly. 'It's safe to come out. Mum and Robin are doing the washing-up in the kitchen.'

I'd left Robin standing on a chair at the sink, a tea towel wrapped round his waist, pretending the spoons were sharks while Mum obligingly made her fingers into people desperately trying to escape. There was a lot of splashing going on and it would take a while to mop themselves and the kitchen floor.

I looked round the room. Many pairs of fairy eyes stared back at me, but none were big and green and sparkling and *real*.

'Bindweed! Don't play hide and seek with me!' I said.

'I'm not deliberately hiding – and you're useless at seeking,' she hissed, though I still couldn't spot her.

'Where are you?' I said, peering round and round.

'*Here*, in this wretched travesty of a house!' Bindweed hissed.

The door was still glued shut on the fairy house, but when I peered through the little latticed window I saw her glowering inside, sitting cross-legged on the tiny crocheted rug.

'My goodness, there you are!' I said. 'Oh, you look so sweet!'

'Stop mocking me! Get me out at once!' she commanded.

'Why can't you get out the same way you got in?' I asked, trying the door again in vain.

'I managed to prise open one of those clumsy windows but, when I squeezed through, the window snapped shut, very nearly chopping my feet off as it did so. And now I can't get it open again and I'm trapped! This is the most uncomfortable dwelling in the world. It's all fake. You can't get into the bed because the sheets are made of plaster. You can't wash in the sink because the little taps don't turn. You can't hang your

dress in the wardrobe because that door doesn't open either. Get me out at once!' Bindweed demanded.

I dithered, circling the house, wondering how on earth I was going to do that.

'Do hurry up! I'm becoming increasingly claustrophobic!' Bindweed said.

I guessed this wasn't a good thing. I tried to puzzle it out. I saw the little window where she'd got in, and saw she'd attacked it with Mum's nail file, slightly buckling both. I had a go myself and managed to get it open again, though it would only stay that way if I stuck my finger in.

'Can you squeeze out now?' I asked. 'Quickly, because it's digging right into my finger and it doesn't half hurt!'

'How can I squeeze out when your finger's totally blocking my exit?' Bindweed grumbled, but she gave it a try.

She climbed up and along my finger, squashing herself paper-flat when she got to the gap, and after several frantic wriggles *just* managed it. The window snapped shut on my finger. I stifled a scream, gritted my teeth and eased it out.

'Oh, that hurt so! Look, I'm bleeding!' I said, examining my throbbing finger.

'That's only a slight scratch,' said Bindweed dismissively,

in between taking great gulps of air.

'And the window's got a bit more broken now, look!' I said worriedly.

Bindweed shrugged. 'Well, it wasn't made properly, was it?' she said.

'How can you be so heartless? Mum loves this little fairy house,' I said.

'It's easy. I don't *have* a heart,' said Bindweed.

'Of course you do. Everyone has a heart. It's what makes the blood go round your body,' I said.

'I don't have any blood either. I have sap,' said Bindweed. She put her hand out and rubbed her wrist on the jagged edge of the window.

'Don't do that!' I said, snatching her hand away. She'd managed to cut it slightly. As I stared, a tiny drop of sticky white liquid oozed out of the little wound.

'See? Sap!' said Bindweed, in a superior fashion.

It really *was* sap, that white sticky stuff that seeps out when you cut a flower stem. I stared at her in shock. She really was a different species altogether. She wasn't a miniature child with stuck-on wings; she was an ancient little alien from Fairyland.

'Anyway, I'm sure it doesn't do you any good to cut yourself. You could probably leak to death. And don't get up to any more mischief!' I said, trying to sound stern. It was difficult giving a scolding to someone about twenty times my age.

Bindweed took no notice anyway. She was sniffing, her pointy nose twitching. 'What's that delightful smell?' she asked.

I sniffed too. 'I think the cakes are ready to come out of the oven.'

'They do smell delicious,' Bindweed conceded. 'I'm rather peckish after all that drama.'

'You'll have to wait till teatime,' I said.

'But I won't be here at your teatime,' said Bindweed. 'I will hopefully be removed to my new dwelling.'

'Oh! Well, I'll see whether Mum will let me have just one for pudding now,' I said. 'Then I can share it with you.'

Bindweed looked at me, rubbing her wrist. 'You're an obliging child,' she said.

It was very scant praise, but I couldn't help glowing.

CHAPTER SIXTEEN

It always seems like ages waiting for cakes to get cold enough to decorate. Robin kept poking them to see if they were still warm.

'I don't see why we *can't* start decorating. I don't mind if the icing goes all runny. I like it when the butter melts into my toast,' he said.

'You have to wait for cakes to cool,' I said.

'*You have to wait for the cakes to cool – cos that's the rule!*' Robin sang. 'Hey, do you like my song? I just made it up all by myself, and it rhymes too!'

He sang it over and over again until Mum and I felt like screaming, but it was such a silly, catchy tune we found

ourselves singing it as we made the icing. Mum had specially bought some little bottles of food colouring. They were red and yellow and blue.

'I think pink would be a lovely colour for fairy cakes,' said Mum. 'We could put a tiny drop of red in the icing sugar and mix it carefully. They'd look pretty, studded with little silver balls.'

'That's too girly,' said Robin, talking out of the side of his mouth in a bad imitation of Micky.

'We could make pale blue icing too. Would you like that, Robin?'

Robin considered. 'I want mine to be yellow! Bright yellow!' he said.

'Oh, like the sun,' said Mum, smiling. 'That's a lovely idea.'

'No, like emojis,' said Robin. 'I'm going to do the winky one. I can make the face out of those coloured chocolate buttons.'

'That's very inventive – though not very fairy-like,' said Mum. 'But you do whatever you want, pet. What do you want to do, Mab?'

'We don't have any green colouring, do we?'

'Well, why would anyone want to make a green cake?' said Mum.

'*I* want to,' I said. 'Well, just on one of my cakes, to see what it looks like. Hey, I could mix a little drop of yellow and a little drop of blue and then the icing would come out green, wouldn't it?'

'I suppose so,' said Mum doubtfully. 'But it would look a bit weird – more like a witchy cake than a fairy cake.'

'Well, it doesn't matter, does it?' I asked. 'You're letting Robin have an emoji cake and that's weird too, isn't it?'

'I suppose I've got to face it: I've got two very weird children,' said Mum. She frowned as she mixed the icing in her bowl, biting her bottom lip.

'Mum?' I said. 'It's all right. We can have plain white icing if you'd rather.'

'No, darling. You can decorate your cakes any way you like. I was just thinking, though – maybe I've gone over the top with all my pretty fairy things,' said Mum. She glanced round the kitchen at the Flower Fairy tea towel and tray, and the Margaret Tarrant fairy pictures she'd bought at a car boot sale. 'Maybe I'm the weird one.'

'No you're not! You're only saying that because Dad mentioned it yesterday. He was just being mean. It's lovely that you like fairies,' I declared. 'And *I* like fairies. In fact, the

minute I finish decorating my cake I'm going to put on my lovely fairy dress.'

'And I like fairies too,' said Robin. 'I'd quite like a fairy dress when it's my birthday. And Fido wants one too, though I'm not sure how I could dress him up in it because his wheels get in the way.'

Robin is *definitely* weird, but the great thing is he doesn't care. He's actually very creative. He made four bright yellow emoji cakes, one smiling, one winking, one sleeping, and one devil one with two little horns made out of slices of chocolate.

Mum made four pink fairy cakes sprinkled with silver balls and hundreds and thousands.

I made four green fairy cakes. I decorated three with pink chocolate buttons. The fourth had little blobs of cream cheese on top. I hoped they looked like white flowers. Then I made leaves with thin slices of cucumber.

'Yuck!' said Robin, wrinkling his nose. 'You don't put cheese and cucumber on *cake*!'

'It's a special savoury cake,' I said.

'It's very . . . inventive,' said Mum. 'Well, we're all going to have a lovely tea.'

'Mum, do you think we could possibly have one now, as a

special treat? It's such a long time to wait till teatime. Please! P-l-e-a-s-e!' I begged.

'All right then,' said Mum. 'Just one.'

'Yay!' said Robin, reaching for his winky emoji cake.

'Thanks!' I said, picking up my savoury cake. 'I'm just going to change into my fairy dress now.'

I dashed into the living room, found Bindweed tweaking the snub noses of three little fairy dolls, popped her in my pocket and carried her off to my bedroom.

'Why did you stop me having fun with those hideous dollies?' Bindweed complained.

'Because I've brought you a special fairy cake,' I said. 'Look!'

I set the cake down on my bedside table and stood Bindweed beside it. She looked at it but didn't say anything. Her head was bent, her long curls hiding her face.

'I know it looks a bit weird but it's meant to be a picture of bindweed. All the white blobs are flowers made out of cream cheese, and the leafy bits are cucumber because I know you like the taste. Still, it's probably odd to put it on a cake. You don't have to eat it if you don't want. I know you're very picky about your food,' I said awkwardly.

She looked up at me. Her eyes were very green and shiny.

'It's a beautiful cake,' she said. 'I love it! You made it specially for me?'

'Yes. It's a goodbye cake,' I said. 'Try a bit.'

She bent forward and took a nibble at the edge. 'Mm!' she said, her mouth full. She swallowed and took another bite and then another and another, circling round the cake. 'It is delicious!'

I don't think she particularly liked the cake itself, but she certainly seemed to be appreciating the topping. I put on my fairy dress, fluffing out the skirts. It still looked ridiculous, and I was worried about people staring at me when I went outside, but I felt I needed to wear it.

I sat on my bed and watched Bindweed circling her cake. She went in and out of focus because my eyes were a bit watery. I knew I was going to miss her terribly. I didn't go and hang out with Robin and Mum, though they called to me. I told them I was busy working on my project. It was actually more or less finished, though I'd left a few gaps in the pages for pictures.

I settled down to drawing now, and when Bindweed sat down at last for a bit of a rest I attempted a portrait of her.

'Wait!' she said, arranging her curls and straightening her

cap. 'I must look a sight! And I seem to have become a little sticky. Perhaps I need another duck ride!'

'You look fine just the way you are,' I said. 'Just try to keep still.'

'I've been squashed flat for many years,' said Bindweed. 'I don't ever want to be still again!'

She stood up, walked to the edge of my table – and then went on walking in thin air! She started somersaulting rapidly downwards. I gasped, breaking the point of my pencil as I rushed to catch her, but she flapped her wings and soared upwards, circling my head.

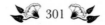

'Bindweed! Stop teasing me!' I said, snatching at her, but she kept darting just out of reach.

She seemed full of energy now, though she'd been so weak before. Clearly the cream cheese and cucumber had been good for her. She flew all the way up to the ceiling, turned herself upside down, and walked across it jauntily.

'Can't catch me!' she called down at me.

I abandoned my portrait, found another pencil, and tried to sketch her rapid flight, but she was quicker than any butterfly and it was almost impossible. She cried out triumphantly and then attempted somersaulting in the air, whirling round and round rapidly, but then she faltered. She did her best to straighten out, but her wings stayed limp and she started falling rapidly.

I caught her just before she hit the carpet and cradled her in my hands. She lay there, quivering.

'Bindweed? Are you all right?' I asked anxiously.

'Of – course – I – am,' she whispered.

'Of course you're *not*!' I said. 'You've exhausted yourself with all that showing off!'

'I felt – so much – better,' she said. 'I went – dizzy for a moment.'

'Well, no wonder! You can't dart all over the place, not

after being squashed flat for so long. You have to take it easy,' I said. 'I don't think you're ready to live by yourself yet,' I added hopefully.

'Of course I am,' she insisted.

'Well, I think you should stay with me another couple of days, perhaps a week or so, just till you're absolutely fighting fit,' I said.

She shook her head firmly, her curls tickling my fingers.

I sighed. 'All right then. But you'd better have a proper rest now, so you've got your strength back by this afternoon,' I said, and this time she nodded.

I tucked her up in the slipper, put it in the dark under my bed, and crept out of my bedroom. I wanted to spend every minute playing with her now that she was determined to leave me, but I knew she really did need to take it easy.

I spent the rest of the morning with Mum and Robin playing an ancient game of snakes and ladders that we'd found at a car boot fair. It was fun to play, but I stayed feeling anxious, wondering how Bindweed was going to cope in the future. What if she faltered and went dizzy when a hawk or a buzzard was flying overhead? What if she was sunbathing in the grass and a rabbit nibbled her green booties? What

if she fell down a badger hole and was mistaken for a tasty snack?

I was so worried now I could barely eat my lunch, even though it was chicken and roast potatoes.

'There, I shouldn't have let you eat that cake,' said Mum. I hadn't eaten so much as a crumb of it, but I couldn't tell Mum that.

'No, it's just that my tummy feels a bit funny,' I said truthfully.

'I'd feel funny if I'd eaten a bright green cake,' said Robin. 'But my emoji cake was absolutely yummy. Can I have another one for pudding, Mum?'

'There won't be any left for tea at this rate,' said Mum, but she let him take one from the tin.

She pulled me onto her lap and gave me a cuddle as if I was as little as Robin. 'What's up, pet?' she said softly, rubbing my tummy.

'I just feel a bit . . . sad,' I said.

'You're thinking about Dad, aren't you?' Mum said softly.

'No, I'm not,' I said, but Mum didn't seem to believe me.

'It's only natural to feel sad that he's got a new family now,' said Mum.

'I don't feel sad about Dad. Well, I do a bit. But it's not that, it's . . .'

'I know,' said Mum. She didn't know, but it was still very comforting to be held on her lap and cuddled.

Then Robin wanted to get in on the cuddle, and clambered onto Mum's lap too, clutching Fido, so it was a terrible squash.

'Watch Fido's wheels!' I warned Robin. 'I don't want them tearing my fairy dress.'

'I'm so glad you like it, Mab,' said Mum. 'I was worried you might feel you were too old for dressing up.'

'I love it,' I said, although the thought of going out in it and everyone staring made my tummy churn more.

It was a really warm sunny day too so I couldn't hide it with a coat. But it wasn't as much of an ordeal as I'd feared. When we set out for the graveyard, a lot of people who were out for a Sunday stroll smiled when they saw me – but not in a mocking, sneery way.

'Someone's going to a party!' said a lady with rosy cheeks. 'Have a lovely time, dear.'

A little girl about Robin's age tugged at her mum's arm and said, 'Look at that girl in the fairy dress! Oh, I want one just like that!'

A grandad gave me a little bow as if I was royalty and said, 'Make way for the fairy princess!'

Bindweed was tucked down my satin bodice. She didn't make a sound, but I could feel her laughing.

Robin looked at me closely. 'Your dress is moving!' he said.

'I've got Nibbles scrabbling about inside,' I said. 'Ssh! Don't tell Mum.'

Robin gave me an elaborate emoji wink. 'Your secret's safe with me!' he hissed out of the side of his mouth.

I kept a careful eye where we were going. I knew this route towards Mum's supermarket. When we got to it, Mum had a quick glance inside the door.

'Are you looking out for Mr Henry?' I asked.

'No, I'm just . . . seeing what's going on,' said Mum. 'I'm not even sure he comes in on a Sunday.' Then she suddenly gave a little wave. I peered inside too, and saw him standing there, looking smart in a blue shirt and cream trousers. He was waving too.

'Hello!' he said, coming to the door and smiling at all of us. 'Are you going up to town again?'

'No, we're going to a graveyard where the dead people live,' said Robin.

'Really?' said Mr Henry.

'It's Mab – she wants to study the gravestones in the church down that little lane,' said Mum. 'I suppose it sounds a bit morbid.'

'Not at all. I like looking at gravestones too. The old ones are really interesting,' said Mr Henry. He looked over his shoulder at the checkouts. 'We're not very busy at the moment, and I haven't taken a lunch break. Do you mind if I come along too?'

'Well . . .' said Mum, going bright pink.

I stared at her. I couldn't read her expression. Was she horrified – or thrilled? She wavered while we all waited. Mum looked round at each of us, and then back to me.

'It's up to Mab,' she said.

'Up to *me*?'

'It's all your idea, going to see these gravestones,' said Mum.

It was mean of her to make me say yes or no. I couldn't say no right to Mr Henry's face – it would look so rude. But maybe it would be easier to slope off and rehome Bindweed if Mum was distracted by Mr Henry.

I shrugged. 'OK, yes – do come,' I said.

Mr Henry grinned at me. He had a lovely smile. I could see why he made Mum go pink. She was smiling back.

Robin was frowning. 'Ooh,' he said, pouting.

'I sense an objection,' said Mr Henry, looking at Robin with his head to one side.

Mum gave Robin's hand a little shake.

'It's not me,' Robin said quickly. '*I* don't mind. It's Fido. He doesn't like strangers.' He pretended Fido was making little growly noises.

Mr Henry laughed. 'Oh, that's easily overcome. I keep a packet of dog treats in my pocket.' He felt around, brought out a totally invisible packet, delved in for an imaginary treat and held out his hand to Fido's old woolly mouth.

'Woof woof woof!' he said, pretending Fido was golloping the treat.

'Fido doesn't talk like that,' said Robin sternly.

'So how does Fido talk?' said Mr Henry.

'He says *woof, woof, go away, I don't like strangers*,' said Robin.

'Robin, don't be so rude!' said Mum.

Mr Henry laughed. 'Well, I'll have to try extra hard with him. Perhaps you could put in a good word for me, Robin.'

Robin was wrong-footed. He couldn't work out what to say, so he stuck out his tongue instead.

Mum looked agonized. 'Robin, that's so naughty!' she said. 'Whatever will Mr Henry think!'

Mr Henry seemed to think it funny. He stuck out his own tongue and waggled it at Robin.

'Mr Henry!' said Mum.

Robin pulled his worst face, wrinkling his nose and pulling his jaw sideways.

Mr Henry pulled an even worse face, making his eyes pop and his mouth entirely disappear.

'Oh!' Robin shrieked. 'Oh, that's so hideous! Show me how to do it!'

Mr Henry showed him, and then pulled another face, this time practically turning into a gargoyle.

Robin shrieked with laughter. Mr Henry did too. They pulled faces all the way to the graveyard, obviously firm friends now.

'You must stop pulling faces now – it's not respectful!' said Mum, as we went through the little cast-iron gate to the churchyard.

'Yes, Mum,' said Robin.

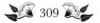

'Yes, Mum,' said Mr Henry, which made Robin burst out laughing again.

Mum sighed. 'You two!' she said, but she was only pretending to be cross. She came up close to me. 'I'm sorry if they're spoiling your outing, Mab. You feel free to wander around and have a good look at everything, OK, darling?' she whispered.

It was more than OK. While Mum and Mr Henry and Robin looked at gravestones at the front of the church, I slipped round the side to the back. It was darker here, shaded by a huge old yew tree that had spread itself widely until it took up half the room. There were really old gravestones, so yellowed with lichen that I couldn't read the writing on them. There were sepulchres too, like little stone houses. The really old ones had great cracks in their sides. They looked as if a skeleton might stick a bony arm through the gap.

Some graves were just grassy tussocks outlined with crumbling brick, though others were grand with marble columns, and there were several angels with their wings permanently spread, watching over us. The grass grew almost up to my knees in this part, so I had to wade through it. The path to the bolted church door was mossy, and the unkempt

grass around the graves was thick with buttercups and daisies – but there was no sign of any bindweed on the grey flint walls surrounding the graveyard.

I could feel Bindweed being tumbled this way and that by my knee action. She struggled until she got her head out of my pocket – and then gave a little cry. She pointed urgently with one small finger towards the thick hedge at the back. Most of it was threaded with dark green ivy – but there were a few delicate strands of paler green too, and big flowers with white waxy petals.

'Bindweed?' I whispered, my heart thudding.

'Bindweed!' she agreed, and she scrambled right out of my pocket and flew to the hedge.

I followed her, tripping here and there, but I didn't dare take my eyes off her. She was there at the hedge, flying from flower to flower, and when I got close up I saw she had tears running down her pale cheeks. She was calling, delving here and there, clutching the long strands of winding stem.

'Where are you, my sisters?' she cried. 'Bindweeds? Please, come and greet me!'

'You won't find any hedge bindweed fairies – they died out years ago,' said a husky voice, and a second small winged

 311

person flew out of the tangled ivy that was choking the hedge. Another fairy! It seemed to be male, a little taller than Bindweed and much stockier, with brownish skin and yellow hair in tight curls that stood out round his head. He had scaly dark green wings the exact shade of the ivy surrounding him.

'You're an ivy fairy!' I said.

He hovered in the air for a moment, staring at me in shock, and then dived into the hanging clumps of ivy.

'It's all right. There's no need to be frightened of her. She won't hurt you,' said Bindweed scornfully. 'She's my girl.'

I felt my heart thumping. She'd called me *her girl* again.

Ivy thrust his yellow curls out of the tangled growth. He peered at me fearfully.

'Bindweed's right. Of course I won't hurt you,' I whispered. I held out my hand to try to reassure him, but he dodged away.

'You can't catch me,' he said.

'I don't want to,' I replied.

'Of course she doesn't,' said Bindweed. 'What would she want with a common ivy?'

'I'd sooner be a common ivy than a practically extinct bindweed,' said Ivy, jumping from leaf to leaf and then turning a somersault in front of her.

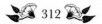

'*Practically?*' said Bindweed.

'Well, there are a couple of little field bindweeds creeping about here and there, though they mostly all got stamped on years ago,' said Ivy.

'There are little bindweeds here? Still? Where are you, my sisters?' Bindweed cried, flying down to the ground and searching frantically in the long grass. 'Bindweeds? *Bindweeds?*'

Something scurried between my feet – one, two, *three* tiny fairies, pink and white with stubby little wings that only lifted them a few inches in the air. They held hands, even when they were flying.

'My own kinfolk!' said Bindweed. 'At one remove, of course.'

'Don't get too excited. They're a timid little bunch. No fun whatsoever,' said Ivy.

Bindweed held out her arms to the tiny pink fairies. They hesitated, looking at each other, unsure.

'I'm a bindweed,' said Bindweed. 'Can't you see that? Come here, you little sillies, and let me hug you! It's so wonderful to see relatives – albeit lowly ones.'

I didn't think her wise to start insulting them when they'd only just met, but they didn't seem to mind. They tottered forward in their funny little pink booties and Bindweed

enveloped them in her arms, hugging them tight.

'You dear little girls!' she said.

The smallest one wriggled free. 'I'm not a girl!' it said indignantly. 'I'm a boy!'

'Dear little girls – and boy,' said Bindweed. 'So do you have special names?'

They shook their heads.

'Then how shall I tell you apart?' said Bindweed. She dismantled the hug and lined them up in size order. The tallest came up to her waist. The middle one was hip size. The little boy only reached her knees. He started sucking his thumb anxiously.

'You can be Pinky,' said Bindweed, pointing to the biggest. 'And you can be Twinky. And the baby can be Dinky.'

'I'm not a baby either!' said the smallest, taking his thumb out of his mouth.

'So there are four of us bindweeds, though I of course am a superior hedge variety. Look at my beautiful big white flowers,' said Bindweed, gesturing. She flew up to Ivy. 'So I rather think we bindweeds outnumber you, Ivy.'

'Oh, you do, do you?' said Ivy. He put his fingers in his mouth and gave a piercing whistle.

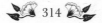

Yellow curly heads poked out all over the place, in the hedge, up the trees, across the gravestones. There was a whole colony of ivy fairies. Bindweed did her best not to look overawed.

'My goodness, you sturdy survivors,' she said, in queenly fashion. 'Oh well, I suppose I'll have to put up with a few neighbours – but no carousing at night, if you please! Come, little fieldies. Let us find a suitable home together.'

She took hold of Pinky's hand, who linked fingers with Twinky, while Dinky clutched her desperately, and they all flew upwards, feet kicking. Bindweed popped the three small fairies into the largest white flower, though its petals were a little overblown. She chose the choicest flower for herself, a perfect dazzling beauty. She nestled into it daintily, giving a little wriggle of delight.

'Oh, the joy of having a fresh fragrant bed at last!' she said. Was she suggesting my slipper *wasn't* fresh and fragrant? I felt hurt, though I could see just how Bindweed blended into the flower so that she was scarcely visible.

'Do you think this is the right home for you at last, Bindweed?' I asked. I spoke softly, but at the sound of my voice the three field bindweeds squealed in terror and all the ivies dived back into their secret dens, though the first one hung in the air, hands on hips to try to look bold.

'I think it is,' she said. She lowered her own voice. 'It's not the most select of areas, but maybe some of my sisters might be tempted to take up residence here when I've colonized it successfully. I will content myself with the three little ones for the moment, though they seem lacking in sap.'

I bent forward until I was almost touching her.

'And you're not overwhelmed by all these ivies?' I whispered.

'I shall soon put them in their place,' said Bindweed.

'They won't hurt you?'

Bindweed snorted. 'I should like to see them try!'

'And what will you do about food and drink?' I asked.

'There will be copious morning dew on every petal and leaf at sunrise,' said Bindweed. 'And salads and fresh fruit and berries.'

'You have to be careful with berries,' I said. 'Didn't you say some of them are poisonous?'

Bindweed sighed. 'I am almost two hundred years older than you, and my kinfolk have been on this earth since the beginning of time. We have been stamped on, trapped in cages, shot at with bows and arrows, eaten by animals and squashed flat in books – but I have never yet heard of any fairy poisoning itself with the wrong kind of berries.'

'All right. I was just checking,' I said, wounded.

'Mab? Mab, can you hear me, pet?' It was Mum calling me from the side of the church. 'Come and have a look at this gravestone!'

'In a minute,' I called back.

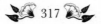

I hovered anxiously beside Bindweed. 'So you're sure you'll be all right?'

'I feel at home here,' she said simply.

'Then I suppose it's time to say goodbye,' I said. My throat felt so tight I was finding it difficult to speak.

'Goodbye,' said Bindweed, with a little wave.

So that was it. I turned quickly so she wouldn't see the tears in my eyes.

'Goodbye,' I mumbled, and went towards the church.

'Wait!' It was only a little cry, but I still heard it distinctly.

Bindweed had her hands on the edge of her flower and was leaning towards me. She was wiping her eyes with the back of her hand.

'Bindweed? Are you all right? You're not crying too, are you?' I asked, running back to her.

'Of course I'm not crying!' she said indignantly, though her eyes were as wet as mine. 'I simply want to say thank you for freeing me from that great book. And for doing your best to look after me. I am exceedingly grateful to you. Would you like one last wish?'

'Oh, Bindweed!' I didn't know what to wish for. I'd got my own back on Cathy. Micky was my new best friend.

 318

I'd met up with Dad again – and I knew now that I didn't want him to come back.

'Hurry up, or I might change my mind!' said Bindweed, though I think she was just teasing.

'I wish . . . I wish I get to see you again!' I said.

Bindweed raised her tiny arched eyebrows. 'That's easy enough. I'm sure you will be able to persuade your mother to bring you here.'

'And you won't mind? I don't want to disturb you,' I said humbly.

'I think I would rather like a visit or two. Now and then. When you see fit,' said Bindweed.

'That will be lovely,' I said.

'It will be even lovelier if you brought a cake with you occasionally. Or a special sweet strawberry?' said Bindweed.

'I'll do my best,' I said.

Then I held out my hand and she clutched my little finger and we embraced in our own fashion.

'Goodbye, my own girl,' Bindweed said huskily.

'Goodbye, my own dear fairy,' I said.

'Mab?' Mum was right behind me now.

Bindweed let me go and flew into the hedge, her wings

flapping so fast she was scarcely visible.

Mum stood squinting into the sunlight. 'Mab! Did I just see . . . ? Am I dreaming? It can't be true, but I'm sure I just saw . . .' she stammered.

'A fairy!' I said, and I hugged her tight.

My Fairy Project by Mab Macclesfield

Do you believe in fairies? I'm sure nearly everyone in our class would say no. Yet if I'd asked that question when we were in Reception I think lots of you would have said yes. Very little children love to dress up in pink sparkly dresses and play with fairy dolls. They skip about like fairies in their ballet class. They love fairy stories and fairy films and fairy games — and nearly everyone hopes the tooth fairy will come at night and leave a coin under the pillow. But as children grow older, they slowly stop believing that fairies are real.

However, some adults carry on believing in fairies. They have all sorts of pretty fairy ornaments and decorations in their homes and go to special fairy fairs. I think this is a good thing. But I think these fairies are pretend, just like fluffy, smiley teddies aren't like real wild bears.

Excellent!

My project is about *real* fairies.

This is a toy fairy.

Great
drawings,
Mab!

This is a real fairy.

There are many more flower fairies. They all like to live outdoors. They like to keep well away from human beings (us).  But there are indoor fairies too. They can  sew and do all kinds of tasks if they feel like it. But they can also be very naughty and play tricks. They can spoil the milk and make a mess and steal things. They are even known to tangle shoelaces.

Very good! ✓

Fairies come in all different sizes too. Some can be as big as us. Some only come up to our knees. But most are very little and could sit in your hand (but they probably wouldn't want to unless they *really* like you).

Great!

There are also fairy animals. Some are very fierce and scary like great big bulls. There are dog fairies who can be scary too. There are cat fairies and even a caterpillar fairy called the Gooseberry Wife.

There are lots of other magic creatures, like elves and pixies and hobgoblins, and boggarts who sound very rude and like to live in cupboards and caves. It would be fun to meet a boggart.

The queen of all the fairies is called Mab. I'm not just saying that because it's my name. It's true. Shakespeare wrote about her in his play *Romeo and Juliet*. He also wrote about Queen Titania in *A Midsummer Night's Dream* but I think Mab is much more fairy-like. Titania is silly and falls in love with a man with a donkey head. Shakespeare also wrote about a hobgoblin called Robin Goodfellow. (My brother is called Robin. Robin Goodfellow is famous for playing lots of pranks. So is my brother.)

There are all sorts of paintings of fairies. They were very popular in Victorian times. Some are very pretty and some are very weird. There's a painting by Richard Dadd called *The Fairy Feller's Master-Stroke* which makes your eyes go funny because you can't quite make out what's going on. It's as if you're peeping through the grass. If you peer really hard you can see Queen Mab in her fairy coach riding across the brim of a magician's hat.

The fairy painter I like best is a man called John Anster Fitzgerald. He painted a portrait of himself having a dream about fairies. It seems more like a nightmare to me, because some of the fairies look like furry demons. There's one pretty lady fairy with a big purple convolvulus flower above her head. These flowers can make you fall asleep or have funny dreams.

They are like the common bindweed, flowers that grow wild and like to coil their way up other plants and choke them.

Bindweed fairies are very magical. If there are any fairies still living now, I think they might well be bindweeds. But it wouldn't be wise to go looking for them. They might easily take against you and give you a big wart on the end of your nose. Or worse. However, if you are kind to fairies they will repay you with good deeds. They might even grant you wishes.

Well done, Mab! I think this is an excellent project. Maybe a real fairy helped you!

Mrs Horsley

Have you read them all?

LAUGH OUT LOUD
THE STORY OF TRACY BEAKER
I DARE YOU, TRACY BEAKER
STARRING TRACY BEAKER
MY MUM TRACY BEAKER
WE ARE THE BEAKER GIRLS
THE WORST THING ABOUT MY SISTER
DOUBLE ACT
FOUR CHILDREN AND IT
THE BED AND BREAKFAST STAR

HISTORICAL HEROES
HETTY FEATHER
HETTY FEATHER'S CHRISTMAS
SAPPHIRE BATTERSEA
EMERALD STAR
DIAMOND
LITTLE STARS
CLOVER MOON
ROSE RIVERS
WAVE ME GOODBYE
OPAL PLUMSTEAD
QUEENIE
DANCING THE CHARLESTON
THE RUNAWAY GIRLS

LIFE LESSONS
THE BUTTERFLY CLUB
THE SUITCASE KID
KATY
BAD GIRLS
LITTLE DARLINGS
CLEAN BREAK
RENT A BRIDESMAID
CANDYFLOSS
THE LOTTIE PROJECT

You might also like

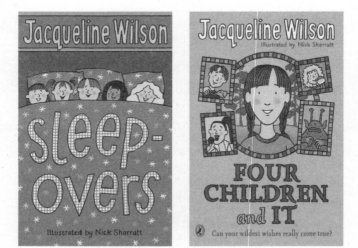

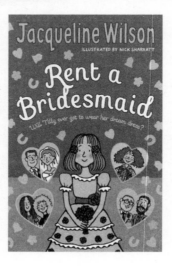